LOST BOYS

SUMMER 1973: BOOK 2

DEAN CADE

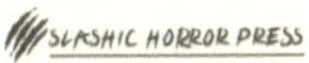
SLASHIC HORROR PRESS

ISBN-13: 978-1-7644884-0-2

Edited and formatted by David-Jack Fletcher

Cover Design by Christy Aldridge of Grim Poppy Designs

Between 1970 and 1973, one of the country's most prolific serial killers murdered at least twenty-nine teenage boys—perhaps many more unidentified and forgotten. The killings, dubbed the Houston Mass Murders, were once considered the worst serial murders in US history.

Summer of 1973 is a fictional account of some of those lost boys.

SATAN'S ALLEY

BILLY FELT THE PAIN in his stomach; the hit of heroin was wearing off. Arms crossed, he shivered despite the summer heat as he walked down the grimy street past unsavory characters and cheap motels. Flashes of the cage returned. Billy grabbed his head. He didn't want to remember. He needed another shot, and fast. A car turned the corner, and for a moment he swore it was the dark red '68 Plymouth GTX. He thought they found him and froze. An ivy green '69 Plymouth Road Runner turned the corner, its driver in shadow, and Billy breathed out.

The image of the man with the fire in his eyes taunted him. He couldn't stop the memories: the hand on his face, the roughness of the board, the handcuffs biting his wrists, and the pain below. Billy smacked his head as he felt the knife cut into his side again. He focused on his breathing and let the images fade. Lifting up his shirt, he ran a finger across the scabby wound and felt blood.

Billy took a shaky breath. He was no longer at the house, on the board, or in the cage. He knew he was free on one condition: he had to deliver on who he promised to them.

A black '67 Chevy Impala pulled up to the curb next to him.

Billy leaned in the window. "Hey man, I was hoping to run into you."

"Get in," the shadowy man said.

"I'll do this date, but there's something else I've gotta do." Billy kept a soft, even gaze.

"What's that?" The man was eager and impatient.

"I need to borrow your car and meet someone in the Heights." Billy kept his hand steady on the door. "It's important."

"I don't know." The man looked out the windshield.

"I'll stay the night with you," Billy offered.

"Alright." The man nodded. "Come on now."

Billy got inside the car and thought, *I'm sorry, Lane, that it has to be you, but I ain't going back.*

PART 1

BSA Lightning

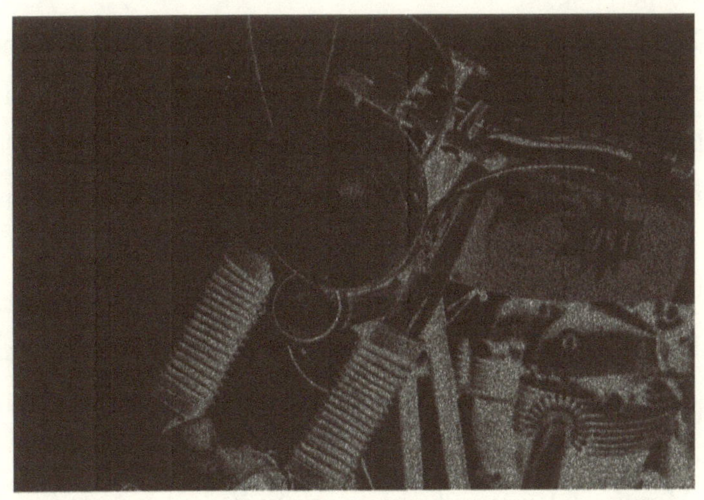

ONE

THE WORLD SPUN IN light and shadow. Lane opened his eyes, and the morning sunlight blinded him, sending swirling patterns into the darkness behind his eyelids. Turning on his side, he opened his eyes slowly and felt another sensation—the harsh dryness of his mouth and throat. He noticed clothes strewn on the floor, realizing some were not his.

The sound of a slight snore grabbed his attention. He turned the other way to see James with the remnants of a black eye, lying naked at his side and wrapped in a sheet that barely covered him. Lane sat up and pulled out of the sheet, feeling the warm summer air from the half-open window blow on his bare flesh.

James stirred, stretching his arms and legs. The movement pulled the sheet the rest of the way off of him. Tentative, Lane reached out and touched James's chest, and he opened his calming blue eyes.

"Morning," James said, groggy but happy as he glanced at the locked bedroom door, then ogled their naked bodies.

"Hey." Lane's heart beat fast.

"Damn, that was one hell of a night, huh?" James slid his hand up Lane's side to his armpit.

Lane cleared his throat to overcome the dryness. "What happened last night?"

"You don't remember?" James smiled a wicked smile.

"Not quite." Lane circled James's hairy nipple with his finger. "I remember it was foggy, and then you were on top of me."

"Well, we made it back here. You stripped off your shirt, saying that you hated the summer heat." James pointed to the clothes on the floor. "I guess you hated those stupid shorts, too."

"How did you get naked?" Lane's eyes widened.

"I said, 'What the hell?'" James moved closer. "And I locked the door, took off my clothes, and wrestled you down."

"No way," Lane said, feeling the warmth of James's body as his excitement grew. *How come I don't remember this?*

"I did it like this." James demonstrated the act by lunging forward, grabbing Lane, and pushing him down on the bed, where he pressed his naked body against his.

Shouldn't I remember this? Lane flinched from the bruise on his abdomen, but his heart beat faster, and he couldn't look away from James's bright blue eyes.

"Then what happened?" Lane whispered, feeling James stiffen.

"We wrestled a bit." James ground against Lane, stirring up trouble. "Then you passed out."

"So, nothing happened?" Lane bit his lip.

"Come on, Lane, you would know if something had happened." James flexed.

"Right on," Lane said, letting James hold his arms back over his head.

"Do you want to do it?" James leaned in, nibbling Lane's ear.

"Yeah," Lane admitted, flexing back.

The alarm clock drilled through the moment, dampening the mood with its mechanical hammer striking the bell repeatedly.

"Oh damn! I've got to go to work, man." Lane pulled away, admiring James's body as he disabled the clock.

James put his arms behind his head, enjoying the attention. "Damn, Lane, you're going to drive me crazy."

Lane tripped as he stood, clumsy yet visibly excited.

"What time do you get off?" James asked, watching him.

"About four-thirty, I reckon." Lane pulled his work coveralls out of the closet.

"Do you want me to come over?" James watched Lane slide a leg at a time into his coveralls.

Arching to slide his arms in, Lane zipped up halfway and looked in the mirror. The sight reminded him of the gas station dream he had of James in the same coveralls, especially since he was not wearing underwear.

Lane looked away from his reflection and grinned. "I do."

"Cool," James said, sitting up in the bed.

"What are you going to do today?" Lane sat down on the edge of the mattress and laced up his boots.

"I don't know." James stood up, confident in his nakedness. "I'll figure something out."

Lane rose, facing him. "I mean about home and stuff?"

"Don't worry about me," James said, standing his ground.

"Oh, yeah." Lane drew closer to him.

James reached out and slid an arm around Lane's waist inside the coveralls, kissing him roughly. Lane kissed him back, and just as roughly, he pulled away, both of them breathing heavily. The moment was taboo and electric.

Biting his lip, Lane said, "You're going to be trouble."

"I hope so." James beamed.

"I got to go," Lane said, not wanting to leave.

"Then go," James said, his eyes daring him to stay.

Lane pulled himself away and said, "Be cool when you take off." He picked up a pair of jeans off the floor and tossed them. "Put something on."

James slipped into his jeans. "See you later."

"Yeah." Lane bit his lip again as he watched James thumb the unbuttoned top of his jeans and trace the happy trail of hair.

"Right on." James copped a sly look as he watched Lane slip out of the bedroom.

Lane shut the door behind him and exhaled. The lock clicked. On the twin mattress in the living room, Kyle held on to Jenny, both wrapped in a blanket. *Why is he still home?* Lane carefully walked past them to the card table, grabbing his billfold and keys.

The Ben Hur complex seemed deserted. Water lapped the concrete sides of the pool with a sloshing sound. The uncommon wind kept the humidity low. Lane stopped and looked back at #19—the apartment sealed from the outside world. He thought of James in his room and wanted so badly to be there.

Wow, this is fast and insane.

Two

Lane turned onto the road. The walk to work felt different that day. He was excited and scared about what had happened the night before. With a little effort, he pushed his ruminations about James to the back of his mind as he continued on to his blue-collar job. Passing Wallace's house, he felt slightly sad not to see the old man's wizened visage on the porch.

Across the street, the Henley house seemed harmless in the daylight, especially without the ominous, dark red GTX out front.

That car freaks me out.

Lane looked down, zipped up his coveralls to a higher position, and felt a chill as if someone were watching him. He walked onward, feeling the gaze of a stranger's eyes on him emanating from the blinded windows.

Memories of fog and someone digging and shoveling sand in the dark crept forward. *Who was in the dunes at the beach last night?* Lane's thoughts drifted, and he realized he was still a little stoned, so he picked up his pace. *I wish I didn't have to go in today.*

The canopy of trees gave way to the morning traffic on Shepherd Drive. Lane passed a torn piece of paper with the letter M. Struck with many rusted nails on a telephone pole, it flapped in the breeze.

Lane psyched himself up and said, "Let's do this so I can get home." Then he thought, *And hang out with James.*

The Mobil Station was open for business, with the garage door cranked up and Jeff working on a gray primer '65 Mustang Fastback inside. Through the dirty glass, Lane saw Ben sitting in the office, sipping a cup of coffee. The metallic Pegasus sign rang in the wind, its red-outlined, winged white horse mocking from above.

Why is the dirty hippie here? Lane stepped toward the garage to answer his nagging doubt, and a bell rang, stopping him in his tracks. A '70 Dodge Van, beige with green and brown stripes along its sides, pulled up to the pump, ringing the bell again as its back tires crossed the line.

A blond-haired surfer leaned out the van's window. "Hey, man, can you fill her up?"

"Sure," Lane said, turning on the gas and putting the spigot in the tank. "You want me to get the windows?"

"Nah, it's cool," the surfer said, leaning back as his stoned girl, with long brown hair and small wire-rimmed glasses, waved.

Lane waved back and checked the rotating digits. He felt the nozzle's flow, and the vibration told him the gas tank was close to full. Before he could stop it, a calloused hand took over.

"Whoa!" The interruption surprised Lane.

"Hey, I got it," Ben said sharply.

"What's up?" Lane asked.

"Don't worry about this, Lane. Just go inside the office and have a seat." Ben motioned with his head.

"Alright, thanks for stopping by." Lane nodded to the beige van.

"Go on," Ben said, adjusting a dirty rag tucked under his belt.

Lane smiled at the surfer. Turning toward the office, he saw Jeff snickering from the open garage bay. His smile faded as his anger rose. Jeff vanished from sight, and Lane felt the heat of the day basking him. *None of this feels right. I'm not late. Hell, I've never been late in the last two years.*

He entered the grimy office—it reeked of old cigarettes—and made a face. Luckily, the door was propped open. Plopping himself down into a greasy chair, he waited, his eyes taking in the small, dingy space. He noticed his dented metal lunch tin on the shelf where he left it on Saturday, making a mental note not to forget it. Through the glass, he watched the surfer and his girl drive off in their shambling beast of a van. Ben waved them away and turned to his office, his shoulders dropping to his sides. Lane could see the years written on Ben's face as he walked in and sat down behind the cluttered desk, folding his hands next to his coffee cup.

"What's going on, Ben?" Lane broke the silence.

Ben met Lane's level gaze. "Times are tough, Lane. You're a fine worker and all..." He sighed, not knowing how to finish the sentence, but the meaning was all too clear.

Lane's whole body tensed, and he leaned forward. "Are you firing me?"

"I've got to cut costs." Ben's eyes squinted tight against the expected onslaught.

"You've got to be kidding me. I've worked my ass off for you, Ben, since I was sixteen." Lane glared with defiance in his eyes.

Ben avoided Lane now and looked out the window. He hated letting the kid go, but he had no choice. "Business ain't so great anymore. I'm thinking of selling the station, and I have Jeff to worry about."

"Screw Jeff! All you are doing is supporting his habit, old man." Lane huffed in his seat, feeling incompetent in a no-win situation. He regretted what he said; everyone had some sort of habit, even him.

"I've cut your last check, and I put a little extra on it." Ben slid a dirty envelope across the scuffed wood.

Lane fought back a tear. "Goddammit, Ben, this isn't fair."

"The world ain't fair. It never has been, boy," Ben said.

"You're just another sellout." Lane shook his head at all his wasted time working as a gas jockey and felt the anger fade. "You at least could've given me time to look for another job."

"I'm sorry, Lane, but I've got to get to work on a carburetor." Ben rose and shuffled out.

"Hey, man, I want my tools," Lane called after him, unbelieving at how he was being dismissed.

"You know where they're at," Ben replied, not even bothering to face him as he moved away from further conflict.

Lane stood up and paced around the small room. He grabbed his lunch tin off the shelf, knocking over some auto part catalogs. Picking them up, he noticed the cash register with its drawer hanging ajar. The dirty green cash tempted him with a promise of instant gratification. He reached forward with caution, then shut the drawer with a sigh. *With my luck, I'd probably end up in jail.*

The garage—so familiar—now seemed alien. Lane ignored Ben and rummaged through the tools, picking out the wrenches he had bought over the last two years. One wrench, three and one-eighths, lay on the oil-stained cement next to Jeff, who was under a jacked-up '67 Mustang Fastback. Lane snatched it, clanging it into his lunch tin with the rest.

Jeff slid out from under the Mustang, his long hair tied back into a dirty ponytail. "Hey, man, I need that to finish up."

"It's mine, and I'm taking it." Lane shrugged and walked off.

"Shit! I can't use the other wrench. It's stripped." Jeff sat up.

"That's too bad." Lane latched the tin, rattling the tools inside. The moment was petty but felt good since Jeff was always mean to him.

"Ben, I need that." Jeff scowled.

"Shut up and get back to work," Ben muttered from the carburetor he was reconstructing, shifting his glasses higher on his nose.

Jeff mumbled to himself and slid back under the car.

Lane observed the garage where he had worked for so long, and he felt the weight of sadness. "It's been real, Ben."

Ben looked up from his work for a second. "I'm going to need that uniform back when you get a chance."

"No way, man." Lane turned his back on the leathery old mechanic and could feel his eyes boring into him. "See you around."

The Pegasus sign bent and whirred in the slight breeze, sounding like a metallic whinny of a horse. Lane glanced at it, remembering his dream as he walked away from the gas station. He unzipped his work coveralls down a third of the way, letting some air in to cool off his sweat-covered body underneath. Absently, he rubbed a finger across his name patch, feeling the stitching. The letters felt soft and worn. It was the third pair of coveralls he had as a gas jockey. He had torn one and grown out of another, but this one always felt right. He felt sad knowing it was the last time he was going to wear it.

Shepherd Drive felt busy with too many cars. The traffic upset Lane's equilibrium. He set off—the opposite way from home—toward 19th Street. *Hell, I better cash this check while it's still good.*

THREE

In a daze, Lane walked out of the cold bank lobby into the sauna feel of summer. He looked down at his arm and wiped a smudge of grease back and forth until it faded. *It has to be some kind of mistake.*

19th Street looked and felt like a forgotten small-town main street. A few shops were open—the cleaners, the hardware depot—but a blight had taken over, leaving the rest abandoned and some boarded up. At the center, a burned-out Heights Theater sat empty behind its charred marquee.

Lane noticed none of it. The interaction inside the bank replayed in his head. Insufficient funds and waiting three days were two of the points the teller had made. He remembered soft classical music playing in the lobby while he waited for a banker in a brown tweed suit and a ridiculous orange tie to tell him more bad news.

"Mr. Bowden, there is more than one signer on these accounts," the banker had said.

"Something is wrong with this—something you're not telling me."

"Sixty-eight dollars and two cents are in the joint savings, and five dollars and forty-nine cents are in the checking," the banker had continued, pointing at the ledger.

"This is fucked up." Lane had fought back his rage.

"There is no need for that language," the banker chastised.

"Okay, close the savings. I'll wait for my damn check and close it too." Lane had felt impulsive and rash.

"I'll waive the fee and get your money." The banker had stared at him like he was trash. "Does that sound good?"

"Whatever, man," Lane repeated out loud, shell-shocked.

The scratching sound of the pen echoed in Lane's mind, recalling how he signed the paper and took the cash. He fidgeted with the lunch tin, rattling the tools inside it, trying to shake off the lousy vibe of the transaction as he walked on.

What the hell am I going to do?

A red Plymouth GTX blared its horn as it rushed by, and Lane instinctively jumped back on the curb. He grabbed his chest, feeling dizzy and faint. The GTX drove off into the run-down desolation.

Was that the same car? Lane took a couple of deep breaths to calm down, feeling the strange remnants of last night's high. *I'm just imagining it and need to eat before I fall down. The little grease pit on Yale ought to do the trick.*

FOUR

Inside the smoky interior of the dark red GTX, the scruffy teenager craned his neck as the blond teenage driver chuckled. The dum-de-dum rhythm of "Easy Livin'" by Uriah Heep played from the car radio as they drove past a bleak set of buildings.

"He's right there." The scruffy teen tapped the glass of the side window as Lane stepped off the curb at the intersection at Ashland Street.

"There are too many people out." The driver adjusted his glasses as he slowed in front of a boarded-up store.

"Why are you stopping?" A manic anxiety filled the scruffy teenager as he watched Lane walk out of sight out the back window. The song fed his tension and his desire to lure the kid in and catch him.

"Patience, man. He's going down there on foot." The driver's amusement from honking the horn faded. "I'll follow him, but you need to be cool."

"Fine." The teen felt his stubbly chin. "Turn around then."

The driver glared, then shook his long hair out of his face and gripped the wheel. The GTX rumbled as it turned onto 19th Street and cruised into traffic. Two blocks down, they caught sight of Lane's back clad in his dirty blue gas jockey coveralls and slowed down.

"I just want to get it over," the scruffy teen hissed between his teeth. "*He* is so riled up."

"You know how he gets. Once he eyes one, there's no turning back." The driver slowed more as Lane glanced over his shoulder.

"One day it will all be worth it," the scruffy teenager said while he stared, almost hoping to make eye contact. "And I'll get out."

"Separate lives. Separate worlds." The driver nodded to the beat, clicked a Zippo, and lit a joint as they watched Lane continue on, oblivious to the danger.

"Yeah, I guess so." The scruffy teenager caught the warning of things better left unmentioned—things that could get him handcuffed to the torture board again. "I let Billy go."

"What the hell?" The driver breathed out a stream of smoke.

"I figured he could get closer than us." The scruffy teen took the joint.

"Does he know?" The GTX jerked as the driver tapped the brakes.

"More or less." The scruffy teenager shrugged. "It doesn't matter as long as he gets to do his thing."

The metal anthem rocked on while they tailed Lane, line of sight blocked by a slow-moving '54 Buick Roadmaster driven by an older lady.

"I think I know where he's going." The driver's lip curled, and he cut the wheel, turning onto a side street.

"Good, I'd rather get him sooner." The scruffy teen clenched his fists.

FIVE

Rounding the corner, Lane spotted his destination, the Yale Street Pharmacy, with a faulty soda fountain and worn grill. He admired the sign, Yale Street Drugs, and noted its irony, considering the state of the Heights. The rumble of a muscle car shut off around the corner while he looked up.

Lane felt a chill as he walked inside, and the glass-paneled door jingled a bell. He wasn't sure if it was the air conditioner or something else and shrugged the feeling off. The place was empty, save for a couple of older men sipping coffee at the counter. He chose a booth by the window so he could daydream about a life that was not his own.

The waitress greeted him in a familiar voice. "Well, look what the cat dragged in."

"Wow, I had no idea you worked here." Lane was surprised to see Tammy in uniform, red hair pulled back, holding a pencil and pad while chewing a broken-in piece of gum.

"You and everyone else." Tammy blew a gum bubble with a loud pop.

Lane asked, "So, how was church?" with a tilt of his head.

"Oh, that was great." Tammy looked to the kitchen, the mostly empty diner, then back to Lane. "Aren't you supposed to be at work?"

Lane downcast his eyes to the table, then looked up. "Old Ben is cutting back, probably closing up shop sometime soon."

"Everything seems to close up around here," Tammy said.

"You're telling me." Lane blinked.

Tammy rolled her eyes and shifted her weight to lean on her other leg. "Hey, is Jenny over at your place?"

"Yeah, I saw her this morning before I left." Lane tried to keep a straight face.

"Good." Tammy sighed. "I've been telling her parents some stories."

"She's safe with Kyle." Lane pushed his lunch tin away from his side.

"You never know with his kind. He's not like you, at least when you're not drunk and handsy." Tammy smacked her gum.

"I'm sorry." Lane felt a wave of discomfort was over him, thinking about their conversation at the drive-in. "I just want to make that clear."

"Okay." Tammy looked him over. "I believe you."

"I promise that was a one-time thing." Lane gave his best puppy dog face.

"Wait a minute, Lane Bowden, you've met someone, haven't you?" Tammy's eyes glinted.

Lane slightly blushed. "Yeah, I guess I have."

The bell jingled, announcing the arrival of some suits and a smartly dressed lady from one of the nearby businesses, probably an insurance company by the look of them.

"Good for you." Tammy straightened her posture when she saw the cook staring at her with a spatula in hand. "What can I get for you?"

Lane noticed the change in tone and appreciated it. "Um... A burger and one of those chocolate shakes should do it."

"I'll get it right out." Tammy winked.

More patrons entered the diner, jingling the bell again.

Crossing, she greeted them. "I'll be right with you. Have a seat anywhere."

Lane's eyes drifted from the booth toward the windowsill, and he thought about his final paycheck. *Everything is going to be okay. I have a little money to tide me over. Kyle owes me, and there are three weeks before the next rent is due. It will work out.*

The curb outside was bare from his vantage point except for the edge of a chrome bumper and dark red quarter panel of a muscle car. He leaned forward trying to get a better view, and Tammy slid a burger and a glass of water onto the table.

"That was quick." Lane smelled the char-grilled aroma.

"I'll be back with your shake." Tammy wiggled. "In a shake or two."

Lane chuckled at her antics. The sound of a motorcycle drew his attention outside the window. A biker rode by, gunning it as he passed. Lane pressed his face against the thick glass for a better view.

The bike slowed and turned around, cruising back to a stop across the street. The rider was James, wearing a leather jacket and looking like a rebel. He nodded and pulled up his dark sunglasses, inviting Lane to join him on the bike.

A heavy milkshake glass clunked on the table, waking Lane out of his daydream as a different motorcycle vroomed off.

"Here you go." Tammy drifted off before he could reply.

Lane glanced from the frosted glass to the window. *Damn it, James, you better come by later.*

The burger was delicious, and the shake was divine. Lane felt refreshed as he judged the contents of his wallet. He stuffed most of his cash in a side compartment and left fifteen dollars in its fold.

On cue, Tammy dropped off the check and read his thoughts. "The shake is on me for the drive-in."

"Thanks, Tammy." Lane left two quarters on the table and got up, grabbing his tin, not noticing the dar red GTX cruise past outside the window.

"I'll see you around, Lane." Tammy grabbed the tab, smiled for a second, and was off pouring iced tea at another table.

It doesn't matter if she knows. Lane looked around and was glad he got to the diner early. Pausing mid-step, he considered aspirin from the pharmacy, but his hangover had mostly departed, so he nixed the idea and headed for the door.

Six

Lane shut his eyes for what felt like just a moment. Opening them, he saw nothing but the road moving under his feet, one step at a time, over concrete. Looking up, he saw the formidable Heights Hospital looming as if it were waiting for another victim. The sun was out, yet there was a gloomy veil of despair surrounding the four-story brick building, like an ancient citadel harboring the threat of pain and suffering behind its high walls. He approached with trepidation, wishing he did not have to go inside, though he knew he must for his mother's sake. He wondered which window on the fourth floor was hers. *Could she be watching me from above?*

The sound of tires over gravel drew his attention to a '70 Cadillac DeVille, and for a second he saw the gold sedan haloed in red as a car passed behind it. The Cadillac turned out onto the street, revealing only parked cars in its wake and the sound of an idling motor in the lot.

This place gives me the creeps.

The lobby was vacant, so Lane picked up his step and crossed to the elevator. He could feel his heartbeat and the chill on his wet skin from the cranked-up air conditioning. As he walked to press the button for the lift, his footsteps echoed off the marble floor. A security guard appeared and motioned toward him. He waved him off and hit another solid button to close the doors and saw the muttering guard turn to confront someone unseen as they shut. Staring up at the moving needle on the floor dial, he pondered how useless security was in these places.

The nurses' station on the fourth floor was barren. With stealth, he made his way inside room 407 and closed the door to any possible outside disturbance. The overhead light was off. Warm sun rays shone in luminescence across the floor in patterns filtered from the leaves of an oak tree outside. The space was silent, save for the science-fiction-style noise of the beeping machines.

The arcing up-and-down patterns of his mother's vital signs appeared in green, wavy lines across the small, black monitor beside the bed. Peaceful and youthful in her sleep, her silky auburn hair flowed out onto the pillow. Lane remembered all the times she was there with a smile, freckles dotting her face, and dimples accenting her loveliness. Her kind brown eyes—now shut tight—were always forgiving of whatever stupid thing he had done.

Lane stepped closer and grasped his mother's hand, feeling the warmth.

She stirred, groggy, and looked around. "Lane, is that you, baby?"

"Yeah, it's me, Mom." Lane felt the grip tighten around his palm.

"I was dreaming about the ocean." She looked like she could see the waves.

"That sounds cool." Lane reached behind him and pulled up a hard-backed chair to her bedside.

She looked him over. "Where have you been? I miss you."

"I've just been busy with work and stuff." Lane looked out the window toward the majestic oak, wishing it were all just a bad dream.

She leaned forward. "Lane, I want to go home."

"Don't worry. We'll figure that out soon." Lane looked away, realizing she had forgotten about selling the house.

"I bet the place is a mess. Did you mow the yard? I mean, it's summer, right?" She looked confused, her eyes darting around the room.

"Mom, you've been here for a while now," Lane said steadily.

"I have?" Her eyes focused. "Damn. I forget sometimes." She grasped Lane's hand tighter. "You have to get me out of here."

"I'm trying. Last time, Doctor Benway wanted to do more tests," Lane said.

"Screw that bastard." She teared up. "I can't believe this is happening to me. What have I done to deserve this?"

"I love you, Mom." Lane felt helpless, too weak to deal with the situation. "It's going to be okay."

She reached back into her mane of hair and felt around. "Are you taking care of yourself, baby?"

"Yeah, everything's cool, I guess," Lane said, shifting in the uncomfortable chair.

"Is that no-good Kyle helping you out with rent?" she asked.

"Everything's fine," Lane said, not wanting to talk about money. *I wish there was a way out, and I could ride off with James, but I'm stuck.*

She looked at the far wall. "Your father came and visited me."

Lane stood up, scooting the chair back. "What? What the hell is he doing here, messing around?"

She eyed Lane and sighed. "I called him."

"Why would you do that?" Lane paced around the room. "He doesn't give a damn about us."

"He's your father, Lane. You should know him. If anything happens—" She broke off as fresh tears flowed down her face.

"Nothing is going to happen." Lane leaned in to kiss her cheek. "You're getting out of here. I promise."

"Oh, Lane, give me a hug," she said.

Lane hugged her close. "It's okay, Mom."

"I'm so scared. Please help me." She broke down.

"I will." Lane pulled away from the embrace, feeling torn up inside and unable to express it.

She caressed the bangs away from Lane's forehead. "You're all grown up now. It feels like it was just yesterday when you were just a baby crawling around the kitchen playing in empty boxes."

"Well, I still play, just not in boxes." Lane smiled to ease the tension.

"One day you'll settle down." She beamed at the daydream. "Do you have a girlfriend?"

"Well, not really." *I might have a boyfriend, though.* "I went on a date Saturday night with Tammy to the drive-in for the Apes movie," Lane offered.

"Tammy? Which one is that?" She mulled it over.

"The redhead," Lane said in a noncommittal manner.

"Oh, so you're seeing someone else now," she said.

Lane felt a shock. "I guess. How'd you know?"

"A mother knows. I hope whoever she is treats you right," she said.

"I hope so." Lane mused. *I really hope he does.*

"Oh, Lane, give me another hug." She reached out with her skinny arms.

Lane obliged then disengaged. "I'm going to find Doctor Benway and see what's going on."

"Tell the nurse to bring me some water," she said, feeling the dry skin on her lips with her tongue. "And some ice cream. I need something cold."

"I'll be right back." Lane backed out of the room.

The air conditioning in the corridor felt colder, and Lane braced his arms across his chest. A nurse in her white uniform, with pulled-back hair wound tight under a cap, had her face buried in a patient's chart at the nurses' station. He approached, his feet padding on the floor, and was about to speak when the door to the stairway clicked shut, startling him.

"May I help you?" The nurse straightened her posture and closed the chart away from his prying eyes.

"I need to see Doctor Benway," Lane muttered, eyeing the closed door and then the nurse.

"Regarding?" The reply was icy and cold, in contrast to her look.

"What's going on with my mom, Ellen Bowden?" Lane asked.

"Oh, I see." The nurse noted the room number and turned to an open file buried on her desk. "I will page him, but he should be back in a moment from rounds, regardless."

Lane read the name tag above her torpedo-shaped breasts. "Thanks, Nurse Sherry."

Nurse Sherry eyed him with suspicion but went back to her work.

"Oh, I almost forgot." Lane interrupted again. "She wants some water and ice cream."

Nurse Sherry glared and closed her current file. "Will that be all?"

"Yes, ma'am," Lane said, edging back.

Nurse Sherry grabbed a water pitcher, switched gears with a fake smile, and went to pour it.

Alone, Lane looked back toward the stairwell door. Something felt off. A tall doctor in a white coat entered the area with confidence, occupied with some printed-out test results. Lane refocused and tapped his fingers lightly on the counter.

Doctor Benway looked up, annoyed at first, but smiled as he read the last bit of information. "Hey, Lane. I'm glad you stopped by."

"So what's going on with the tests?" Lane wasn't sure he wanted to know.

"We did a radionuclide brain scan, and from the anterior angle we found what could be a tumor in her right frontal lobe; the bleeding has stopped for now." Benway folded his arms across his chest.

"Can you get rid of it?" Lane's eyes widened.

"Maybe. The only way to see what we're dealing with is to have a surgery and do a biopsy." Benway put his hand on Lane's shoulder. "This is serious, Lane. The outcome may not be good."

Lane asked, hopeful, "If you do it, she has a chance?"

"There are no promises, but if we don't do anything, she is going to die." Benway moved aside as Nurse Sherry returned to the station. "Once the blood tests are back from the lab, we can prep her for surgery."

"Don't cut out on her, man," Lane tried to sound tough.

"Hang in there." Benway nodded, straightening and returning to his paperwork.

Lane wanted to say something else, feeling like there were a thousand questions with no sensible way to ask them. In a daze, he walked away, grabbing an ice cream off a meal cart left outside another room. Behind him, the stairwell door opened.

Inside room 407, Lane found his mom sitting up on the bed, staring at the oak tree outside the sterile environment. "I got you some ice cream. I didn't think they'd bring you one," he said, breaking her trance. "It's chocolate."

"Aw, that's my favorite." She looked younger for a moment.

"I don't want you to worry," Lane said. "We should know something in the morning."

"I know it's going to be all right. There's nothing wrong with me." She opened the small container of Blue Bell Ice Cream and grabbed a spoon from a tray on her bedside.

"There is one other thing," Lane said in a soft voice but decided not to finish.

"Oh, this is delicious. Thank you for this." She devoured a few bites in rapid succession.

"Slow down there, or you'll get a brain freeze." Lane lightened up, watching her.

"Maybe the ice cream will freeze this thing inside my head." She giggled, putting a hand to her mouth.

"Wouldn't that be aces?" Lane felt content for the second time that day.

She set the empty ice cream on the tray and tried reaching into the drawer on the hospital nightstand.

"What do you need, Mom?" Lane was over to her side.

"Can you get the photo album out of the drawer?" She watched him dig through admission papers.

Lane handed over the dog-eared album and sat on the edge of the bed. "Who brought this up here?"

"Wallace came by yesterday. He said you were at the beach." She sighed, looking off into the past. "I miss the beach. It would be so nice to be sitting in the sand with a piña colada."

"Yeah, we went to High Island. The water was really nice," Lane said.

"Wallace is such a gentleman." She thumbed through the book, flipping pages.

"I dig him. That reminds me, I better get his ice chest back soon." Lane pointed at a picture of himself and his mom at the beach. "I look so skinny."

"Remember that day you wouldn't stay out of the water? I had to drag you away," she said.

"I was only six, you know, and the ocean was cool," Lane said.

"Now look at you all grown up, but you'll always be my little boy," she said.

"Okay, Mom." Lane shook his head.

"Always," she said, touching the picture. She was growing tired, her breaths a little heavier, her eyes dreamy.

"Who is the guy with short hair?" Lane leaned back and listened to his mom discuss past times and warm memories. *I like hearing her reminisce about how things were before I knew the truth. Moments like these are golden, not yet lost to time.*

His mother fell asleep, the album on her lap open to a picture of his father, John, on the beach. Lane gently eased the book away and pulled the sheet up, covering her.

Quietly, he walked to the window to watch the majestic oak as it guarded his resting mother like a sentinel. Lane took a deep breath and crossed the room, gazing fondly at his mom, who looked young and peaceful in her slumber.

The hospital room door clicked shut as he left.

SEVEN

LANE SHIVERED IN THE cold, empty corridor as he walked to the elevator in a mild shock. *I can't believe this is happening to her.*

He noticed the nurses' station was barren again as he hit the button to go down. The lever to the stairwell moved while he wondered how he would take care of his mom if she made it or what he'd do if she didn't. Lost in thought, he didn't see the door slowly open.

A bell rang, and an orderly brought an elderly patient on a gurney out of the elevator. Lane moved to go around and felt a hand on his chest.

"We have more coming up." The orderly motioned with his head. "Take the stairs."

"Okay." Lane looked at the unconscious old woman with an oxygen mask over her face, then toward the closed stairwell door. He wanted to protest, but the gurney rolled on.

The door opened into a yellow-lit stairwell with chipped paint over stone walls. It felt tight and made Lane feel claustrophobic. He stepped inside, the door closing behind him, and breathed out.

Several steps down, between landings, he heard a faint rustling. He leaned over the rail and saw darkness. A bulb was out. Lane rubbed his fingers together. *I don't like this.*

The rustling sound came from below, mixed with another sound that he couldn't quite make out. Lane froze and listened.

A scratchy voice whispered what sounded like, "Lane."

No way. Lane bolted to the door, coming out on the second floor. He avoided running into a gurney with a bandaged patient wheeling by. Muttering an apology, he rushed to the end of the hall for a different stairwell and took the steps two at a time. The outside door slammed open into a brick wall as he backed away from the 1920s facade of the hospital building.

Lane waited for someone to follow, straining to hear. The piercing shriek of an ambulance scared him, actually making him jump back. The siren blared on as Lane got a handle on himself. *It was probably just a wino in the stairway. I've got to quit freaking myself out.*

EIGHT

OUTSIDE, THE HUMIDITY INSTANTLY dampened Lane's skin as his panic drifted away with each step from Heights Hospital. He took an alternate route home up Yale Street, following the rising blocks. The moment mattered, and at that moment, Lane needed some groceries for the barren apartment refrigerator. On the corner of Harvard and 23rd Street, the Yates Grocer was small but carried the basics, and it was cheaper than others.

A fear of being penniless and broke crossed his mind, but he shrugged it off as he went inside. Lane set down his lunch tin before walking through the understocked aisles to pick up staples such as milk, bread, ground chuck, bologna, chips, potatoes, Corn Flakes, oranges, bananas, and even some Night Hawk TV dinners. With his arms full, Lane went to the checkout and gave a brave smile.

Mrs. Yates looked him over from behind her wide glasses, her hair put up in a gray bun, and a sensible long dress. "Well, well... I have not seen you in my store in a long while."

"I've had a lot going down lately." Lane lowered the cornucopia onto the counter.

"I know, poor Ellen, bless her heart. You tell her my prayers are with her." Mrs. Yates rustled open a couple of brown paper bags.

"I will." Lane took a long moment to pull a ten-dollar bill out of his wallet and felt a pang for the four dollars left in sight.

"Are you still staying with that Steiber boy?" The register clicked under her apt fingers.

"Yep, with Kyle." Lane remained noncommittal.

"Oh," Mrs. Yates said, clicking her tongue on the roof of her mouth. "How's that working out?"

"Just fine, ma'am." Lane pivoted. "Say, how much are those oranges?"

Mrs. Yates looked over her glasses for signs of a story. Not finding one, she eyed the bag of citrus fruit. "Forty-five cents for the bag, hon."

"I'll take them," Lane said.

Mrs. Yates fumbled with the five pounds of fruit, tilting her head in thought as it settled in a bag with the other groceries. Lane worriedly eyed the lone bottle of milk, wishing she would finish with the register, but he knew she was recalling some gossip to test him on.

"Don't forget the milk," Lane said.

Absently, Mrs. Yates put the milk in the bag, clicked in $1.39, and said, "It's such a shame about that Winkle boy and his friend David."

Lane pictured the telephone pole with the flyer—*Someone had torn it down*—and its reward for the missing boys and nodded. *All that's left is a torn paper and the letter M.*

"His mother has been going out of her mind with worry." Mrs. Yates shook her head.

"Yeah, I can imagine." Lane eyed the groceries. "I saw one of those posters just the other day, in fact."

"I told her those boys aren't coming back from wherever they ran off to." Mrs. Yates put her hands on her hips. "Plain and simple."

"I don't know what to think about all of that." Lane shuffled in place. He remembered the dusty green '68 El Camino sitting behind the Long John's with school books and a pack—right out in the open on the front seat—and he firmly decided not to mention it.

Mrs. Yates clicked her tongue. "It's reckless for boys that age to be running wild on the streets."

Lane held his tongue, then asked, "How much do I owe you?"

Mrs. Yates totaled the order with a sniff. "Nine dollars and sixty-eight cents ought to do it."

Lane pocketed the change and grabbed the sack and his tin, ready to disengage.

"Swing by here and give me a holler if you find anything out about where those boys went," Mrs. Yates called after him.

"Sure thing." Lane hit the door, mumbling, "Nosy old hag."

Nine

Lane headed up Harvard Street for the walk home. The bungalow houses seemed abandoned. The heat had driven everyone indoors to a fan, or, if they were lucky, air conditioning. The double-bagged paper sack's contents shifted with the uneven walk. Lane peeked in and saw the perspiration coming off the glass milk bottle, hoping it would not spoil. Sweat dripped down Lane's underarm, sliding in rivulets across his bare flesh underneath the coveralls. *Nobody's home. I should smoke a joint and nap till supper.*

A low rumble of an engine startled Lane out of his relaxing plan. He turned to see the dark red '68 GTX speed up, then pass him. Half a block up, it U-turned, stopped, and waited with its motor idling.

"What the hell?" Lane said.

The GTX rumbled forward a couple of feet and idled again.

Lane stopped cold. Unsure of which way to go, he waited for the first move of the car. The grocery sack slid from under his arm. He repositioned the bag with the tin on one side to free up a hand. I don't want to fight, not today of all days.

Someone pressed down on the gas pedal, and the GTX's 383 engine revved up louder while unseen eyes watched.

I should run. It was a crazy thought. Lane gauged his surroundings: to the left was a chain-link fence, and on the right was a long dash across the street to a house.

The driver popped the clutch and threw the GTX in gear, peeling out and leaving black tracks on the hot pavement.

Damn, I'm going to get jumped. Lane stood frozen as it raced past him, hot exhaust blowing through his hair and coveralls. He exhaled, watching it speed away and out of sight. *I wish I had a knife.*

The street was quiet, except for the sound of the wind in the oaks.

Was the car at the beach last night? The sloshing sound of the shovel digging in the sand came back to Lane, chilling his sweaty, trembling skin. *No way. Don is probably in that car. They were just messing with me, or else they wouldn't have taken off.* He continued his trek on Harvard at a faster pace, trying his best to shake it off—and failing—and took a right on Aurora Street to change it up, just in case the GTX came back.

Tony wandered around the corner and into view. Thinking fast, Lane walked into some oleander bushes, knocking loose some of the pink flowers and finding refuge in the green pointy leaves. Tony was still wearing the same clothes from the beach and looked dirty, with oily, matted hair. Lane watched and hoped he was invisible. *The last thing I need is for that freeloader to crash my day.*

From his vantage point in the bushes, he saw Tony dig into his pockets, searching for a lighter for a cigarette he pulled from behind his ear. In the background, the dark red GTX slowly cruised around the corner, coming right toward an oblivious Tony. Lane thought about warning him of the danger but decided against it. The muscle car was closing in. Lane watched in morbid fascination as Tony turned to face the idling beast while backing farther into the foliage to conceal his frame.

The red GTX idled with its driver in shadow. Wayne Henley awkwardly stepped out of the passenger side, brushing his bangs away from his intense eyes. Tony greeted him, shaking his hand. There was a perceptible change in their demeanor as the unheard conversation took a turn toward the unfriendly.

What kind of trouble is he in? Lane watched Tony get into the backseat of the GTX.

Wayne looked toward the bushes for a second. His upper lip lightly twitched before he got back into the passenger seat, hidden behind smoky, tinted glass.

The GTX revved up and took off, prowling Aurora Street.

Those cats freak me out. Lane inched out of the bushes, feeling disturbed by the situation. His skin itched from the oleander oil secreted from the rigid leaves. Adjusting the paper bag again with a tighter grip on the tin, he set out at a faster pace to turn onto Yale Street with the firm belief that the more public, the better.

The blocks passed in no time, until he turned off onto 27th Street, glad to not have to pass the Long John Silver's with the abandoned El Camino behind it. His nerves felt shot.

Wow, I need to shake off this vibe. The joint at home sounds cooler by the minute. Tension ebbed away with each step, and by the time Lane saw the sign for his street, Rutland, he felt much better.

TEN

THE 383 ENGINE RUMBLED loud in the stillness and revved higher as the blond teenager shifted the gears of the GTX, speeding up. In the backseat, Tony watched the Heights pass by and felt the tension. He glanced at the rearview mirror and saw the scruffy teenager grinding his jaw.

"You have no fucking idea what you've messed up," the scruffy teenager said.

"I don't get why you're mad. It's Brother John and Maurice that got busted at the beach." Tony's leg bounced. "I got away, and you know I'd never talk to the cops."

"It's not that." The scruffy teen looked to the silent driver, then back to the mirror. "You've seen things."

"Look, I just want to re-up and get some more goofballs. I don't care about the syndicate stuff." Tony hoped he could score and get out.

"What do you know about that?" The scruffy teenager turned around, facing Tony between the seats.

"It's some kind of pornography ring." Tony swallowed. "That's what he does, right?"

The scruffy teen lunged, grasping Tony's throat in his hands. "Don't ever talk about that!"

"Stop." Tony choked, overpowered by the viciousness. "Stop. I can't breathe."

Tony kicked the back of the seat as he saw spots in his vision. Hands clutched his throat tighter, and he could feel thumbs pressing into his esophagus.

"Calm down, Wayne." The driver eyed the neighborhood. "Not here."

The dark hate faded from Wayne's face, and he let go, scratching his scruffy chin.

Gasping, Tony said, "I don't care what you do to them." He backed into the corner of the GTX, putting as much distance from Wayne as he could.

"That's good." Wayne patted Tony's leg and smiled. "Now, tell me where Lane Bowden lives."

"What?" Tony looked bewildered, glancing at the bespectacled driver whose eyes never left the road and then back to Wayne. "I don't know where Lane lives. I just see him around."

"I don't think I believe you," the driver muttered as he cut the wheel to a freeway ramp and floored the gas pedal.

"Where are we going?" Tony felt trapped in the backseat with no way out.

"We're taking you to re-up. That's what you wanted, right?" Wayne moved his jaw around, fighting back an inner tension.

"Yeah, I guess so." Tony's voice rasped, and he coughed.

"Maybe we'll show you something else while we're there." Wayne stared at him in the mirror.

The driver leaned over, bangs hanging down, and clicked on the radio. "Gotta have some jams for the ride."

Black Sabbath's "Paranoid" filled the interior with its distinctive metal vibe.

Tony felt his neck, and fear rose as he realized he might not be able to talk himself out of this situation.

ELEVEN

Lane arched his back, stretching as he walked past the pool in the familiar Ben Hur courtyard. He noticed the pay phone receiver was off its cradle and took a second to right it on the way to climb the cement and iron stairs. He turned the key in the lock of #19. Upon opening the door, stifling, stagnant air greeted him. One-handed, he moved aside a sheet curtain and opened the nearest window. The apartment smelled of sweaty bodies and something decaying in the trash. Holding his breath, he set the groceries and his tin down on the kitchen table. He grabbed the offensive trash bag and set it outside the front door.

Back inside, he put the groceries away. The sweaty milk went in the refrigerator with the meat and other perishables. One of the fridge's crisper drawers stuck open, offset by the weight of the Lone Star. He leaned down and fixed its track, noticing that shutting it caused loose beer cans to resettle on top of each other. Lane stood up and placed the TV dinners in the iced-over freezer. *Even with new groceries, this fridge is bare.*

Kyle burst through the front door, catching his foot on the trash bag. He cursed as he kicked it to the side.

"Whoa!" Lane exclaimed.

Kyle's expression changed on seeing Lane's curious look. "What's doing, Lane?"

"Not much." Lane tilted his head. "What are you doing home so early?"

"I was going to ask you the same thing."

"It's been a hell of a day, man." Lane sighed. " Money is going to be tight for a bit."

"You lost your job?" Kyle looked concerned.

"Ben fired me," Lane said.

"What about rent?" Kyle eyed something across the room.

Lane chose his words with caution. "I told you I took care of mine, but I need your half, especially now."

"Oh yeah, I'll have it by the end of the week." Kyle tapped his foot, his body language impatient.

"Why are you home?" Lane asked.

"I just needed to grab something on my lunch break." Kyle's foot tapped faster.

"Isn't it a little late for lunch at that metal shop?" Lane asked.

"Well, I didn't get to go eat earlier," Kyle explained.

A crash made Lane jump as TV dinners fell out onto the kitchen floor from atop a small glacier inside the freezer. Lane stooped to pick them up. Using the metal side of one, he carved out a spot in the ice for the rest. In the moment, he noticed Kyle had taken the opportunity to snag something off the bookshelf and return to where he was with his usual swagger.

"I'll see you later, Lane. I got to run." Kyle moved to leave.

"Hey, Kyle, we got to talk things over." Lane moved away from the fridge. "Some heavy stuff went down today."

"How about tonight?" Kyle thought fast. "Me and Jenny are going out to that pizza parlor by her house, over by the airport. Maybe if you find a ride, you could meet us."

"Alright, but it might be James since he's stopping by later," Lane said.

"Really?" Kyle raised an eyebrow.

"Yeah, we could ride there on his bike."

"Sounds good." Kyle did not sound convinced.

Lane felt a strange intuition as the door shut. He waited until he could no longer hear footsteps, then eyed the shelves where Kyle had taken something. Books on astrology, mechanics, and Kurt Vonnegut stood out in disarray at first glance. Instead of investigating, he walked to the window to watch Kyle drive off in his super-blue '70 Challenger. *Why was he here?*

The apartment reeked less, but he still slid open the window in his bedroom. He thumbed through his records, settling on Pink Floyd's *Obscured by Clouds*. The needle hit the groove of the track, and the music slowly ramped up, setting the mood.

Rummaging through his underwear drawer, he found the stash he was hoping would still be there; in a loose plastic bag was a lone joint. Back in the kitchen, he lit it off the stove burner, careful not to singe his hair. The first hit was bliss, and he held it in, feeling the stress melt away and satiating his desire to chill.

The lit joint hung loose on Lane's lips as he opened a third window behind a sheet in the living room. The bookcase caught his eye again. Illustrated on the front cover of a book—an off-kilter edition of 2001: A Space Odyssey—was a space station similar to the one he dreamed about. Images of that dream—the promise of James and chaos—filled his head with distraction.

Lane bent down and removed a few books, and a blue pill rolled across the shelf, stopping at his hand. Rotating it between his fingers, he moved some more books out, discovering Kyle's stash: an assortment of pills, uppers, downers, and a few that he could not identify. *I guess he's not loading trucks anymore.*

The realization of Kyle dealing hit hard. *Goddammit, why did you lie to me? I would've understood unless there's something else you're not telling me.* Lane put the shelf back the way it was, wishing he had left it alone. Pacing around for a moment made him tense, so he stretched out on his bed and let the images of the day float through his mind.

Dream I

IN AN ORANGE SPACESUIT that clung tight to his body, Lane floated in the void of space. He was in awe of the many striking shades of blue against the deep blacks and constellations in endless patterns. A strange, otherworldly aloneness washed over him—lost in the vastness of it all.

Lane's bubble-shaped helmet with its panoramic visor made outer space feel off-kilter and dangerous. A white cord, like an umbilical tube, tugged from an attachment to the space gear on his chest. Lane turned to see where it went, and it went deep into spacetime, where the black hole once churned. Taking a deep, controlled breath, its sound amplified inside his helmet, Lane pulled the cord toward him. Someone was on the other end. The cord slacked and looped as the minute figure grew more prominent.

James, clad in a similar orange spacesuit, grabbed a hold of Lane, who felt the slight pressure through the Teflon sleeves. Lane grabbed a hold of him, and together they orbited each other in a slow spin.

Galaxies, and the glory of the universe, whirled around in a breathtaking panorama. James's lips moved, and Lane felt frustrated as he tried to understand through the interference of the helmets. So close to James, it drove Lane crazy not to hear his words. He knew there was meaning, if only he could understand it.

TWELVE

"WHAT ARE YOU SAYING?" The sound of Lane's own voice woke him, and it took him a moment to shake the strange dream fragments from his mind. The index finger and thumb of his right hand were sore from a burn. Absently, he rubbed them together. Downward, he saw a small, charred mark where the joint had landed and burned out to almost nothing.

The turntable's needle skipped over and over on a bump. The repetition created a popping and hissing sound from the speakers. Lane stood, stretched, and crossed his bedroom to flip the record and play the other side of the Pink Floyd album. His mood was melancholy, and the music amplified the feeling.

Stifling, hot air blew in through the window. Lane leaned outside, looking over the courtyard. There was no sight of James's motorcycle, or even Kyle's muscle car. Lane reached inside his coveralls and adjusted his crotch, and he decided in that moment that he might as well wear them for the rest of the day.

Rummaging through the refrigerator, he tossed the hamburger meat on the small kitchen table. He tried shutting the crisper drawer that stuck out half an inch and was full of Lone Star. It did not budge, so he pulled the whole drawer out and found four bottles of beer stuck behind it.

"Jackpot," Lane said with a smile, despite his moodiness. He cracked one of the found beers on a cabinet handle. "And it's Budweiser too." I wonder what else Kyle is keeping from me.

Lane mused as he inspected a frying pan on the stove, finding it clean enough. The burgers slowly sizzled with the click of a burner. The smell of frying meat was delightful, and the music settled, but it was the rumble of a motorcycle that brought a true smile to Lane's face.

Outside in the lot, James sat atop his '70 BSA Lightning. He throttled it once, noticed Lane watching from the window, and shut it off. Beaming, he dismounted and bounded for the stairs, still wearing the jeans and shirt from the day before.

Lane turned the stove burner low and walked into the living room in time to hear James's heavy footfalls echo on the concrete steps. He opened the door, and all the worries of the day faded away. They looked at each other for a second. James reached out, giving a full-bodied hug and a rough pat on the back, and Lane went with it.

Backing off, Lane fought the magnetism. "What's doing, James?"

"I'm feeling lucky to find you at home." James maneuvered around Lane to enter the apartment.

Lane shut the door, feeling his heart beat faster. "I wanted to um—" James's blue eyes distracted him way too easily.

"You don't have to say it." James swallowed and exhaled. "I snuck back and got my bike, and I've been thinking about it all day."

"What do you think I'm going to say?" Lane asked.

James's eyes widened, then relaxed. "Well, I don't know now. Maybe I should just shut up."

Lane stepped closer. "Nobody has to know, right?"

"Nobody, but you and me," James said, moving in closer.

"Good," Lane said, biting his lip, "because you've got me all messed up."

"Do I?" James asked, close enough to touch.

"Yeah, you do, more so than anybody I've met." Lane felt the warmth of James's body.

"That's cool, man." James smiled, puzzling over something in his head.

"So, are we hanging out tonight?" Lane asked, changing course.

"Yeah, I'd like that," James said.

"One condition." Lane's face lit up with a smile. "Take me on a ride on your bike."

"No problem. I'll take you anywhere you want to go." James sniffed the air. "Smells good."

"Oh damn, I'm going to burn the meat." Lane broke away to the kitchen, calling out behind him, "You want a burger?"

James followed and sat down at the small table to watch Lane flip the patties. "Did you put one on for me already?"

"Nah. I always cook two at once, but you can have one." Lane looked James over. "What did you do today?"

"Well, I got the bike and—" James brightened as a Budweiser slid across the table. "Thanks, man." He took a long drink to loosen his tongue. "I've been thinking all day. We hardly know each other, but you're cool on so many levels."

Lane put the spatula on top of the stove, opened the cabinet above it, and placed a yellow and white bag of Lay's potato chips on the table to share. "What's on your mind?"

"I need a place to crash for a while. My old man ain't going to let me back in. He's been looking for a reason to kick me out ever since school ended," James said, laying it all out.

"I would have to ask Kyle." Lane set out a couple of plates and grabbed the pan, sliding a burger onto each one. "Some messed-up stuff went down today."

"What's that?" James clenched his jaw, ready for the blow.

"I lost my job." Lane grabbed the catsup from the fridge and handed over a loaf of bread. Sitting down and facing James, he said, "The old bastard fired me this morning."

"Not because of me." James felt his stomach knot up.

"No, I made it on time." Lane ate a chip, and then he said, "He was going to do it, anyway."

"I've been saving up my lawn money, and I can help out with rent and stuff." James threw it out in a hopeful way.

"Really?" Lane felt hope for the financial prospects. "That would be amazing."

"How much does Kyle pay?" James asked.

"Not enough, man." Lane shook his head.

"He is paying you, right?" James peered across the table.

"Until lately." Lane shrugged.

Over a bite of burger, James said, "Just tell me what you need me to do, and I will help you." He swallowed. "I will help us."

"What the hell!" Lane decided. "Kyle can deal. You can stay here with me."

"That's totally cool." James saw a way out of his dilemma.

"I hope I know what I'm doing," Lane said.

"It'll be fine." James's spirit lifted.

They shared a silence as they ate, both lost in the moment.

"Let's go get my stuff." James chewed over the last bite.

"Right now?" Lane felt incredulous.

"There's no better time than when he's not there," James reasoned.

Chewing, Lane mumbled, "Let's go then." He tilted his head, watching James. *Moving him in is crazy, but maybe it could work.*

Thirteen

Lane followed James across the courtyard to the BSA Lightning, watching him mount and kick-start the bike with ease. He breathed in and looked around to see who was watching. Finding no onlookers, he straddled the bike, feeling awkward being so close to James in public.

"Put your arms around my waist," James ordered, above the vroom of the engine.

"Alright." Lane obeyed, holding on tight as they took off.

The warm breeze buffeted his blue coveralls as he rode on the back of the bike, and it felt sublime on his bare skin underneath. Lane felt firm muscles below the white T-shirt and wondered what James was thinking. Nevertheless, he was content for the first time in a long time.

The turn onto Yale from 27th Street was sharp, and the ride felt exhilarating as James opened the bike up, weaving in and out of the sparse traffic. James elbowed Lane as they cut off an old cowboy, who swerved his rusty white '56 Ford truck to the side, honking its horn in a fit. They both laughed at him as they raced on. Lane held on tighter as James sped up. The worn road tested the motorcycle's shocks. On a sharp turn, they almost took a tumble, but James righted the bike, saving their legs from road rash.

Breathing heavily from the rush of the ride, James waited for Lane to back off the seat so he could flip a leg and dismount. He cut the motor. "We have to walk the bike from here, so I can get in and out quick."

"Is your old man home?" Lane looked ahead to the bungalow house for signs of trouble.

"I hope not." James pushed the bike forward in neutral; its tires made a continuous pop and rub noise over the asphalt.

"Are you going to be long?" Lane asked.

James smiled at the nervous look on Lane's face. "Nah, it should be cool."

"If you say so." Lane felt the tension compound in a strange way as the bike rolled past the drainage ditch that marked each side of the gravel driveway.

"Look, on Mondays, he always goes to the dive bar next to the refinery," James said.

Lane gauged the size of the bike. "Do you have a lot of stuff?"

"Just one bag." James flinched as a rock popped out from under the tire and skittered loudly across the drive. "It's already packed."

"Really now?" Lane gave James an inquiring look.

"No, it's not like that. I...um... I always keep one packed, if you get my drift." James shrugged.

"Oh—" Lane broke it off, not knowing what else to say.

They stopped at the end of the driveway by the chain-link fenced-in backyard, feeling fortunate for no human contact. White linen sheets swayed on dual wire clotheslines stretched high on homemade poles across the grass.

James put his motorcycle under Lane's control. "Here, take it."

"Well, hurry up. This is freaky." Lane took over the weight of the bike.

James looked like he wanted to say something else but instead said, "I won't be long. Just chill."

"Go on, already." Lane motioned to the house with his head.

Unlatching the metal handle on the gate without making a noise, James closed it back. Looking in the yard for something and not seeing it, he opened the back door and slinked inside.

Repositioning his hands on the handlebars, Lane turned the bike around for a quick getaway if necessary. Gravel popped louder under the tires in the stillness. The driveway remained clear as he stopped and waited. One of the larger sheets flapped hard. Lane breathed out, hating the vague feeling of anticipation—fear of the unknown—that was washing over him. *James is taking way too long.*

A black and tan dog lunged, barking, jumping, and pawing at the chain-link fence, causing Lane to jump back.

"Shush, boy, shush." Lane tried to calm the vicious dog with the tone of his voice, but the animal sensed the fear beneath and kept barking.

The dog was relentless. Lane began moving the bike away, and the back door slammed open. James's mom grabbed the dog's collar and turned her fierce gaze on him. For a moment, she stared, sizing up the intruder. Lane stopped rolling the bike and froze.

Rising, she kept a firm hold on the barking dog. "Well, you must be one of James's friends, or maybe you're stealing his bike."

"No. I um... I'm waiting for him to come out," Lane said.

She retied the sash on her robe as she glanced back. "So, he's here then."

Lane nodded, trying to figure out what to say. Coming up with nothing, he shrugged.

A hippie chick came to the rescue in a sheer brown top, flower-patched jeans, and hair braided back in a long ponytail. "Who's the hunk?"

"I'm Lane."

The hippie chick came closer to the fence.

James's mom glared, then asked her daughter, "Have you seen James?"

"No, I haven't seen that loser." The hippie chick wrinkled her nose.

"Well, your brother is in the house, so maybe you should go get him." The dog barked some more, and she got a better grip on its collar. "Quiet down, Max."

The restless canine calmed, and Lane avoided eye contact with it. Instead, he eyed the back door in anticipation. *Hurry up, James.*

A younger, freckled girl in a floral smock and blue bell-bottoms bounced out of the open passage with a shocked expression. James's mom sighed and reached up to feel her wet blonde hair.

"You're hurting him," the girl said.

"Max is fine." James's mom twisted the dog's collar, motioning to the fence. "We have company."

"Hi." Lane struggled to hold the bike upright in the drive.

The three stared at him for a long moment, and he remembered the sisters' names, Jan and Theresa. Before he could speak, the phone rang loudly, sounding like an emergency call, and James appeared in the doorway, to his relief.

Jan rushed past him. "I got it. It's for me."

"Jan's got a boyfriend." Theresa looked faux innocent.

Breathing out, James's mom found her patience. "Honey, why don't you take Max and chain him up, then go inside so I can talk to the boys?"

"Aww, Mom," Theresa whined as she took the dog collar, and Max licked her face in welcome. She giggled and led the dog to a tree with a pawed dirt rut around it. "Can I have some Jell-O?"

"I don't think it's ready yet. Go watch some TV until I come back inside," she said, watching James approach.

"Hey, I just came by to pick up some stuff." James shifted a U.S. Navy duffel bag on his shoulder while his little sister went around him to the door.

His mom sighed and walked closer. "Your father can be mean, but he loves you."

"Not now. We got to split." James looked at Lane and rolled his eyes.

Lane looked down and felt the cool metal of the motorcycle's handlebars. Unsettled, he peered up and saw her whispering something in James's ear.

"No, everything's going to be fine. He's not like that." James curled his lip.

Lane raised his eyebrows and kept quiet.

"I worry about you, James. You can't hang out with trash. Do you know what happens to boys like that? They end up in juvenile hall or even prison," she warned.

"That won't happen. I'm going to stay at Lane's apartment here in the Heights, and I'll call you, okay?" James kept his voice reasonable.

"You do that, and I'll try to talk some sense into your father," she said.

"Good luck with that." James opened the latch and stepped on the crunchy gravel. "Come on, Lane, let's get out of here."

"Bye, ma'am," Lane said, watching her wipe a tear away from her cheek as she rushed into the house, shutting the door.

Max barked again, rattling his chain on the tree.

"Well, that was fun," Lane whispered.

James kick-started the BSA Lightning, revving up its engine. The sunlight reflected off the chrome, brightening the yellow streak and black paint.

"I'm sorry, man. I should've snuck back by myself. I wasn't thinking," James said.

"It's cool. Messed up, but cool." Lane strapped the duffel on his back, tying it tight, as he straddled the back of the bike.

"She thought you were a doper," James said, turning his neck.

"That's just great." Lane shook his head. "It's probably my dreamy eyes, right?"

"I told her you're one cool cat." James revved the engine. "And I like your dreamy eyes."

"I need a beer now," Lane said into his ear.

"Me too, brother." James looked back at his house and sighed.

Lane grabbed onto James's waist—even tighter than before—out of fear of toppling over from the extra weight. James squeezed the throttle, peeling out the back tire on the gravel. The thrust sent rocks flying and clanging into the chain-link fence as the tire caught traction and the bike sped off.

FOURTEEN

THE GRAVEL OF THE Ben Hur parking lot tumbled as the BSA Lightning rumbled to a stop, leaving the hot summer feeling to engulf the boys. Lane struggled to get the Navy duffel off his back. James helped him pull one of his arms free, and then the bag went down with a thump to the lot.

"What do you have in there? Your whole room?" Lane licked his dry lips.

"Nah, just my stuff." James picked up the duffel. "You ever go swimming in that pool?"

"Sometimes." Lane eyed the cool, beckoning water lapping its sides. "Why? You want to?"

"Yeah, I do. Let's put this stuff away and go swimming." James smiled, and it was contagious.

"Alright, if we're going to do this," Lane said, heading up the steps, "I should show you where to put your stuff."

"I was just here." James heaved the Navy duffel.

"It's different now that you're staying." Lane fit his key in the lock and swung the door in.

James eyed the living room carefully, seeing a twin bed center-piece with some bookcases on its side in the darkness of the heavy sheets and a card table topped with a black-and-white television.

"It's kind of a mess," Lane said, seeing it differently now.

"Is this all Kyle's?" James asked.

"Most of it." Lane eyed the dingy room. "We hang out and watch TV and get high sometimes."

"I guess I'm staying in your room," James said.

"When I talk to Kyle, I can ask about moving stuff around in here," Lane offered in a half-hearted way.

"It's cool. I don't want to intrude on his space." James nudged Lane and shuffled to the bedroom.

Lane followed him into his familiar domain. *Wow, the world really has changed since I woke up.*

Dropping the duffel, James sat on the edge of the bed. "This will work." He tested the mattress springs.

"Are you cool with this? I can make you a pallet on the floor if you want," Lane offered.

James looked at the dusty wood floor, then back at Lane. "You're not keeping me like a pet, man."

"You dork. I mean when Kyle is here." Lane tilted his head to the side.

James stood back up and breathed out. "The lock works good, right?"

Lane checked the knob. "Yep, sure does."

"Then it's cool." James looked at the closet and opened it. "My bag will fit in here. Do you think I can use one of your drawers?" He motioned to the dresser.

"Sure, let me move some things around." Lane felt strange deciding space issues.

Digging into a middle drawer, Lane pulled out some blue jeans and shifted them down to the drawer below, revealing a black-and-white picture of a shirtless male in tight jeans.

"What have you got here?" James reached in, grabbed the magazine, and read the title, "Physique Pictorial."

Lane instinctively tried to yank it away. "It's nothing, just a bodybuilding magazine."

Pages flipped open in the struggle, and James asked, "Are those guys wrestling?"

"Give it back," Lane said, "before you rip it."

"You're a freak." James teased.

Lane punched James in the shoulder and let him take the magazine. "No more than you."

James thumbed through the pages of sweaty athletes, stopping on one in the buff. "Damn! Is this what you check out at night?"

"Shut up." Lane felt the warmth of the room close in on him.

"I'm just saying." James moved closer.

"We should go swimming." Lane changed the moment.

"Yeah, we should, but I'm saving this for later." James tucked the magazine under the jeans and sorted some clothes from his pack, settling on the small, red gym shorts.

Lane laughed. "I can't believe we have the same damn shorts."

Pulling his shirt off, James tossed it on the bed. "Come on. Don't be shy now."

Lane unzipped his blue work coveralls, kicked his boots off, and stepped out naked. "I never said I was shy."

Appreciating the view for a moment, James slid out of his jeans with a sly smile. "Neither am I."

The moment seemed to last forever as they checked each other out; their fading bruises added toughness to their physiques. Slowly, they changed into their respective shorts, which were way too short. James saw him, and Lane felt at ease with his own strange desires for once.

"You ready?" Lane asked.

James stepped in close, taking in Lane like a cool drink of water. "You have no idea."

Hearts beat faster as they glanced at each other's free-swinging shorts.

"Come on, James, before you get us in trouble." Lane grabbed James's arm and led him out of the room.

A macramé hanging on a passing wall caught James's eye. "What's with that?"

"It's sentimental. I made it in a class with my mom when I was a kid," Lane said.

James gave him a pseudo-troubled look. "I see."

"Come on, there should be some towels in here." Lane opened the dank bathroom cabinet, grabbing some white terrycloth ones.

"The shower, is it? No tub?" James made a face at the grime.

Lane did not notice the dirt, moved closer, and said, "If you want to soak, you've got to jump in the pool."

"The shower's cool," James said.

"Here you go." Lane handed over a towel, and their hands grazed. Hormones raced at the touch and proximity of skin to skin.

"You want a beer?" Lane asked, feeling funny being so close.

"Yeah." James breathed out.

Lane walked away with James close behind, the magnetism strong. The fridge gave up the last two Budweiser bottles. Lane snapped the tops off a kitchen drawer handle and handed a beer to James.

"Cheers." Lane toasted.

"Right on." James drew close again.

Bottles clinked, and then they both swallowed a gulp of beer.

"I really appreciate this." The sincerity rang true in James's eyes.

Feeling an assortment of contrary emotions, Lane said, "Let's go swimming before you get all queer on me."

"I'll show you what queer is, boy." James reached out.

"I bet you will." Lane dodged out of the way and cut to the front door.

The sunlight was blinding. Lane squinted as he rushed down the hot concrete steps. The door slammed behind him, and James gave chase.

"Ouch, ouch, ouch!" Lane guided his calloused feet carefully across the gravel lot.

"Damn, it's hot." James hopped ahead, opened the gate, and snatched Lane's beer, setting both bottles down.

"Cannonball!" Lane yelled, balling his legs underneath his body, as he jumped into the deep end with a walloping splash.

A tan and red blur greeted Lane as he surfaced, and the splash engulfed him in a deluge. Treading water, he splashed James in the face when he rose.

James spat it out. "Okay, chill out, man."

"Right on, this feels so good." Lane leaned back and paddled, floating up and matching James's position on the pool's surface.

"It does indeed," James said.

The rumble of a passing car's engine disturbed the tranquility.

"Do you remember seeing a car in the dunes?" Lane asked.

"Yeah, I do," James said.

"I've seen that car cruising in the neighborhood." Lane waved his arms underwater to stay afloat.

"No way." James kicked his feet, softly churning the water.

"I swear it's the same one, a red '68 GTX with a hardtop," Lane said.

"We both were high, and it was dark." James paddled his sinking feet upward. "How do you know for sure?"

"I've worked at a garage for a couple of years now. I know cars," Lane said. "Anyway, I saw Tony get in that car this morning."

"Did they see you?" James asked.

"Not really. I didn't want to deal with Tony, so I hid in some bushes before the car drove up." Lane felt the itchiness of the oleander leaves. They did see me before, though.

"That's funny." James grinned.

"He was arguing with Wayne Henley, the guy Don knows," Lane said.

"It's just doper stuff," James said, dismissing it.

"If that's true, why were they digging in the dunes?" Lane heard the sound of the shovel in his mind.

"No. That's creepy, and we were high." James's blue eyes widened.

"It just weirds me out," Lane said.

"Don't think about it, just chill," James said.

"I dig it." Lane breathed out, letting go.

James closed his eyes and said nothing.

The cool waters surrounded Lane and James's lithe bodies as they floated, taking in the sun with the assurance that they were like souls outside the chaos of the world.

"James… What, uh, I mean… What have you done before?" Lane stuttered.

"What are you talking about?" James replied.

In a lower voice, Lane asked, "What have you done with a guy?"

"Some things, not a lot." James looked sideways at Lane. "Just stuff."

"I've only thought about it," Lane admitted. "Until what we did in the ocean and this morning."

"Well, tonight I'll get drunk, and you can do whatever you want to me." James looked around at the empty complex and added, "As long as I get to do the same to you."

"Alright, if I'm drunk too." Lane felt his heart beat faster. "Anything?"

"Anything and everything, Lane. I'm game." James blushed a little.

"Aces!" Lane grinned, and he reached over and dunked James, who, not expecting it, swallowed pool water.

"You're going to pay now." James lunged and pushed Lane under to have him pop back up in his arms.

They stayed that way for a moment, then moved apart, self-conscious of their surroundings.

"I can't believe you've moved in after a day. What the hell was I thinking?" Lane shook out his wet hair like a dog.

"Trust me, it'll be fine." James's blue eyes soothed. "I'll show you some things."

"Things, huh?" Lane smiled, despite his nerves.

"Things… Trust me." James swam to the side and pulled his body out of the pool. His dripping wet shorts clung tight. He grabbed the beers and sat on the side, offering one.

"Thanks." Lane took the beer. "So I was thinking tonight that we'd go meet Kyle and Jenny on the South Side to talk things over."

"And you'd rather see him first than have him walk in on us," James said, his upper lip curling at the thought.

"I just want him to know what's up," Lane said.

James frowned. "Is he going to be cool?"

"I'll handle it," Lane said.

"Fine," James said, taking a drink.

"And then—maybe, if you want to—we could go park behind the airport and watch planes and stuff," Lane added in a nervous prattle.

"That'd be awesome." James kicked in the water and said with a wistful look, "I'd love to see the airport at night."

"Yeah, me too." Lane's excitement grew. "I brought it up since they're going to be at this pizza parlor down there."

James stared far away, imagining it. "You and me, behind the airport."

"Yeah, you and me." Lane inched closer and leaned back, look-ing up at the oaks, the blue sky, and the few clouds beyond.

James closed his eyes. "Ah, that's more like it."

Young and free, they felt the moment.

FIFTEEN

THE BLACK AND WHITE television flickered in the smoky living room from its metal stand against the wall. The sound of Victoria Winter's voice emanated with the eerie music of as she narrated the opening of the gothic horror show.

Tony tried to control his breathing, sitting on a shabby green couch next to the scruffy teenager, Wayne, who stared enrapt at the program. Tony's leg bounced as he looked from his silent captors to a woman in a cell on the television. The scene changed to a nervous guy pacing, holding a hammer as he looked at a picture of the vampire Barnabas. The words "I can't do anything; he has too much power" echoed from the screen.

Waves crashed onto the rocks behind the title, Dark Shadows, to the tune of an electro-theremin. A faux bay window shone light on the blond, bespectacled teenager as he lit a joint.

"Hey, are we cool, man?" Tony asked.

"Sure." Wayne grimaced at the interruption, then smiled.

The blond laughed, coughing out smoke as he adjusted his glasses.

"When can I get that stuff?" Tony licked his lips.

"As soon as he gets back." Wayne shrugged.

"Here, man." the blond teenager passed the joint, his bangs moving with the motion.

Tony's anxiety grew. He sensed that time was running out.

A door slammed in another room, and the man clad in his HL&P uniform entered with a suntanned teenage boy stumbling behind him wearing a goofy grin.

"I found him hitchhiking," the man said in a pleasant manner, depositing the boy on the couch between Wayne and Tony.

"Wow! I think I'm fucked up," the teen slurred.

"You sure are." Wayne scooted over.

Tony watched him dig a small key out of his pocket and close his palm around it.

The man's eyes burned, the fire rising within. "Come here, a sec," he said to Wayne.

"Whoa... This is a trip." The hitcher gazed at the image of the vampire in a coffin intercutting with the trapped woman.

Tony heard the eerie sound of the theremin as he checked out the teen whose head hung down, dark hair dripping sweat, enthralled with the television. He eyed the man in the corner as he whispered with Wayne, and the man's gaze locked on him. The eyes freaked him out, and he looked away.

The hitcher mumbled, "Give me a hit," and the blond passed him the joint.

"What's your name?" Tony asked.

The bespectacled blond answered, "It doesn't matter what his name is."

The hitcher shrugged, trying and failing to pass the joint back. The blond took it from him and hit it, laughing at the situation.

"Whoa..." The teenage hitcher fainted, mouth open with a thin stream of drool on his chin.

"Hey, Tony." Wayne broke in. "He's going to hook you up and give you a ride home."

Tony rose, and the suntanned teen lurched off his shoulder and slumped over. "What about him?"

"He'll be fine." Wayne passed by to sit on the couch next to the boy.

The music caused Tony to shudder. Wayne held up the boy's limp hand and waved it as he chuckled. Tony turned, and the man's eyes felt like they were staring into his soul.

"Come with me. I want to show you something," the man said, drawing him in with the timbre of his voice.

"Okay." Tony felt hypnotized and followed the man through the kitchen and out a door into the garage.

A lone bulb illuminated the center but left lots of space in shadow. A dirty white '65 Ford Econoline van took up half the space. The door shut out the eerie music, and Tony gulped.

"Wayne says that you've been asking about the syndicate," the man said, stepping closer.

"I... I um... I guess so." Tony stepped back.

The man nodded, in control. "You see, I help out troubled boys—boys like you."

"Like when you used to give out candy," Tony said, moving back more.

"Yeah." The man closed his eyes and smiled. "This is different. The syndicate is looking for male models."

"That's cool." Tony felt the garage light dim as he looked into the fiery eyes.

The man rubbed two fingers down Tony's chest. "You think you'd be interested in that?"

"I'm not right for that kind of stuff." Tony shook his head. "I just want to re-up."

"I don't have any of that kind of candy." The man's fist clenched.

"I'm sorry to waste your time. I should go." Tony backed into a large cage and flinched.

The man moved into the darkness, his hand roving along a shelf of tools. Tony looked inside the cage and saw blood and felt mortal fear.

"You don't know anything, but I think you know too much," the man said from within the shadows.

"I don't know what you do, and I don't care," Tony said, panting. "You can trust me."

A hammer swung into the light, and Tony's eyes widened as it smashed into his temple. Sparks flew in his vision, and he felt warm blood flow down his face.

"I think I'm going to keep you around for a while and see if that's true." The man opened the cage and shoved Tony's twitching body inside. It was all so easy.

Sixteen

The motorcycle hummed down the Gulf Freeway, leaving behind the city and its tall buildings as the road roared by in a streak. Lane felt at home on the back of the bike, with James in control. Behind, the sun set as the highway led them into the night, and the first stars appeared, moving overhead in the faraway heavens.

The hum of the BSA Lightning vibrated Lane, causing him to hold on tighter. James leaned forward and opened up the engine with a squeeze of his fist, and pure joy spread across Lane's face from the force of the speed. James turned in profile, taking it in.

The moment was sublime, and Lane felt a sense of rapport. *If he asked me to go right now on this bike and never look back, I would.*

The motorcycle's handlebars were low, causing James to lean forward even more as he sped up. Lane leaned forward with him on the padded seat. His foot slipped, and his ankle touched the hot tailpipe, causing him to flinch. The burn barely touched his glee.

The BSA Lightning rumbled past an eighteen-wheeler, the heat of its exhaust tangible as they passed. The driver blew the truck's horn, giving off a deep blast. Lane looked over his shoulder and raised a fist, making a pulling motion for the driver to do it again. Another blast from the semi rewarded his hand action, and Lane laughed in the wind. The motorcycle left the big rig behind and weaved between two sedans of different makes: a dark green '68 Olds Cutlass and a '72 Lincoln with an orange and white roof. Open-mouthed drivers and riders blurred by.

Over the wind, James yelled, "How much farther?"

Lane put his mouth toward James's ear, feeling the sting of James's dark hair whipping his face. "Take the Edgebrook exit!"

"Okay, hang on!" James pushed the bike to the max.

Lane tightened his arms around James's waist and looked up at the approaching and passing streetlights spaced every so many yards, dimly lighting the freeway. Attached to steel poles, the illumination came from curved arms with elongated eye-like bulbs on stalks. The strange design reminded him of a movie he saw on his old television called War of the Worlds. The attacking Martian ships had the same design, but instead of a yellow light, they would emit a red and yellowish death ray. Lane imagined one of those lights disintegrating a car into dust, and wondered at the strangeness of his mind. *I wish I still had a color TV.*

"Is that it?" James yelled, turning back slightly.

"Yeah, turn here!" Lane felt the G-force abate as they slowed down.

The exit was sharp, and James cut across to the far lane at a rapid pace. Luckily, the feeder road, parallel to the Gulf Freeway, was barren of traffic.

"Make a right at that Mobil Station," Lane said over the engine.

James slowed down and turned the corner. On the right, pine trees formed a miniature wood, and on the left, the destination lay behind the gas station. He glided the motorcycle into the parking lot and ambled to a stop beside the pizza parlor. An assortment of trucks, muscle cars, and even a van filled the Pizza Hut lot. Parked at the far end was Kyle's super-blue '70 Dodge Challenger, looking impressive under the yellow light from the hut thatching of the sign.

Muted light shone through the odd-shaped windows of the brick building, while the night above was in full effect, with a rich, dark blue sky sprinkled with tiny lights. Warm, muggy air blew on a faint breeze, causing pines to rustle in a melancholy way.

The wind triggered Lane's mood. "Let's get this over."

"It's going to be cool, right?" James leaned the bike on its kick-stand. "Hell, you know what I mean."

"I'll bring it up." Lane swallowed and tried to fix his windblown hair with one hand. "Just follow my lead."

"You want me to get your back?" James smirked.

"No, it's not like that, but Kyle can be freaking moody," Lanes said.

"Jenny is here, right?" James bit his lip.

"Yeah, so?" Lane peeked in a window.

"Then this'll be civil." James pulled Lane back. "Quit acting like a Peeping Tom."

"Hey, cut it out." Lane broke free of the grasp. "Civil, huh?"

"Lane, I'm with you. It'll work out," James said.

"You're right." Lane felt lost in James's blue eyes for a second. He shook it off, said, "Let's do this," and pushed open the heavy wooden door.

The smell of pizza was overwhelming and mouthwatering. Random eyes stared as they entered. Similarly dressed as James in work boots, jeans, and a T-shirt—a blue, two-tone ringer versus a tan and brown one—Lane felt self-conscious. James nudged him along, ending the perceived awkwardness.

Curiosity satisfied, the diners went back to their business of eating and drinking in the privacy of their booths around the sides of the brick-walled pizza parlor. The lit-up jukebox in the corner played the opening riffs of "Twentieth Century Boy" by T-Rex.

Lane and James walked past the salad bar and a few scattered tables.

"There they are." James pointed out.

Kyle stared at them agape with a piece of pizza in one hand, chewing, while Jenny waved them over.

James whispered, "He looks surprised."

Lane ignored and led, glad the music was loud enough. He stopped at the edge of the booth and said, "We made it."

Kyle finished chewing. "What's doing, Lane… James?"

"Not much, just riding around on my bike." James stepped to the side.

Lane tilted his head. "I told you we'd stop by."

"I know." Kyle chewed the rest of his mouthful of pepperoni and cheese.

Jenny stood and hugged Lane. "It's so cool to see you."

"Hey, Jenny," Lane said, hugging her tight, "you too."

"Hi, James." Jenny waved.

Uncertain, James waved back. "Looking good, Jenny."

Jenny blushed a little and swayed. "Thanks."

Kyle stood up and puffed up his muscular build in a blue button-down shirt. "Come sit over on this side, babe." He emphasized her place by patting the high-backed seat of the booth.

Jenny slid in and kissed Kyle on the cheek. "Sit down, guys, and join us."

Lane motioned for James to go first and watched him scoot across the brown plastic seat to the irregularly-shaped window. Red-and-white checkered tablecloths that matched the partial curtains gave the restaurant a homey feel.

Lane relaxed on the soft cushion until he saw the look on Kyle's face. "Sorry to bust up your date, man."

Kyle looked around the booth. He glanced at Jenny twirling her hair and James looking out the window. His gaze settled on Lane. "Nah. I told you where we were going to be. So, what's the deal?"

The uncomfortable moment changed when the waitress stepped up. She wore a red shirt with checkered sleeves. Her hair, pulled back in a green visor, travelled far down her back. The gang looked at her, and she asked, "What can I get you, kids?"

"We're fine." Kyle motioned with irritation.

Lane looked at the paper table menu, tracing his finger along the red writing, and said, "A pepperoni pizza ought to do it."

The waitress scribbled on her pad and asked, "Anything else?"

James piped in, "A pitcher of beer too."

Jenny rattled the ice in her red plastic cup.

"I'll get you a refill too, sweetie," the waitress said, slipping away.

Kyle sipped his beer and turned. "What's the story with you two?"

Lane breathed out. He looked from the contrasting faces of James—dark hair, somewhat bruised skin, and blue eyes with a hint of mischief—to Kyle, a sandy blond with the angular face of an all-American jock with emerald eyes. Both of them seemed curious about what he had to say.

"We, um, we have a proposition for you," Lane said.

"Oh yeah? What might that be?" Kyle asked.

Jenny slurped the remnants of her Coke as she watched them intently.

"You know how pissed off James's father was the other day?" Lane began finding his footing.

"So?" Kyle's eyes widened, and he shook his head as realization sank in. "No way."

"My old man kicked me out," James blurted out.

"The place is pretty small, Lane." Kyle clenched his jaw.

"Here you go." The waitress set down a heavy glass pitcher filled with beer with a thud, along with some empty cold mugs and another red cup of soda for Jenny. "Your pizza will be right out."

Before anyone could acknowledge her, she turned, swooshed her long hair, and was off to another booth.

"He's got money to pitch in, and with my job situation, we'll need all we can get," Lane bargained, knowing that rationality might work.

"You'll hardly know I'm there." James hoped he wouldn't be homeless. "I can get food and stuff, too."

"Let him stay, Kyle." Jenny looked like she wanted to spill a story.

"Ah, dammit, I can't see it." Kyle clenched his jaw again. "For one, where's he going to sleep? I ain't sharing my room."

"You don't have to." Lane felt a strange discomfort wash over him.

"I can crash with Lane." James looked up from pouring a beer. After a beat, he added, "On the floor. It's no big deal."

"Maybe after we—" Jenny started.

"Not now, Jenny." Kyle cut her off, and he grabbed the branded matches out of the ashtray on the table. "Come on, Lane. I'm going to smoke outside."

Lane shrugged at James. "Alright, I'll be back."

"I'll try to save you a beer," James joked.

"You better." Lane's smile slipped as he caught Jenny watching him.

Jenny smiled her own secret smile. "Don't worry. I'll keep your new roomie company."

Lane questioned the exchange in his head while he followed Kyle's broad-shouldered gait through the pizza parlor. Distracted by a little boy picking cherry tomatoes out of the salad bar and eating them, he barely caught the heavy door as Kyle went through. He glanced back at the booth. James and Jenny were laughing. It killed him not to know what they were saying.

"Come on," Kyle said from outside.

"I'm coming." Lane caught up.

The night air was warm.

Kyle walked to the side and struck a match, lighting a cigarette.

"So what's going on?" Lane asked.

"It feels like the country out here." Kyle exhaled smoke and looked around, lingering on his prized possession at the far end of the lot.

Lane took in the lone pizza parlor amongst the pines and the brilliant sky above. "Too bad it won't last."

Lights twinkled nearby from a neighborhood tucked in the trees, in contrast to the freeway and the progress that it brought.

"Nothing does." Kyle took another drag, inhaling the bitter smoke and breathing it back out. "I'll have my half of the rent soon."

"Money is not the issue." Lane swallowed. "James really needed a place to crash. That's all."

Kyle raised an eyebrow. "Does that mean we can split three ways?"

"Yeah." Lane felt wary. "What the hell am I gonna do without a job?"

"Something'll come up, man." Kyle shrugged.

"Like it did for you." Lane threw out there.

An edge leaned into Kyle's voice. "What are you talking about?"

"Nothing. It just seems like you get all the breaks," Lane said.

"No more slacking, I promise. I just need to divvy up what I've been trying my hand at," Kyle offered.

"Like dealing or something?" Lane asked.

"Something like that." Kyle stared. "You know what it's like in the neighborhood."

"Damn, Kyle, I do." Lane breathed out. "What if you get busted?"

"Not a chance." Kyle took a drag of smoke.

"We've got to hang on to what we have," Lane said.

"Right on," Kyle said, grinding the butt out under a boot heel.

Lane peeked through the elongated window that spilled yellow light onto the pavement. Then he said, "That's why I think James can help."

"He better not turn out to be some kind of thief or a freak," Kyle warned.

"No, he's down to earth." Lane's eyes drifted to the yellow, black, and chrome body of the BSA Lightning motorcycle.

Kyle tilted his head, trying to figure him out. "We'll see how this goes, but I won't stand for any weirdness."

"Let's go back inside." Lane turned toward the door.

Kyle grabbed Lane's arm, stopping him. "You're like my brother, but I'm warning you."

"I get it, and it'll be fine." Lane felt unstable at the rough contact.

"Alright, but it'd be a lot cooler if Tammy was moving in." Kyle let go.

Lane punched Kyle in the arm. "That's only because you want to see her naked."

"True." Kyle smirked, picturing it in his head.

Lane shifted his weight from one foot to the other. "I'm hungry, man."

"Then go on." Kyle shoved Lane like brothers do.

Lane glanced at the splotch of red that amplified the BSA Lightning logo on the motorcycle and was still unsure of how things were going to play out.

Inside the pizza parlor, James and Jenny seemed to be having a good time without them, as their banter was raucous. Lane wondered if they were talking about him but brushed the idea aside as Kyle brushed past him.

Kyle plopped down on the thick plastic seat cushion. "What's so funny?"

"Oh, James is such a hoot." Jenny snorted.

"We're just funning around," James said, chuckling. He caught Kyle's innate seriousness and asked, "So, is it cool if I stay?"

Kyle grabbed his beer mug. "Yeah, it's cool, I guess."

Lane settled in beside James. "Awesome."

Perking up again, James said, "Don't worry, I'll do my share. I'll even get the tab for the pizza and stuff tonight."

"Thanks, James. That's so sweet." Jenny scooted closer to Kyle.

"Thanks, man," Kyle muttered.

"That's cool." Lane felt everything was going to work out. "See, we make a cool gang."

"If you say so." Kyle sipped his beer.

"Have a beer, Lane." James poured out a pint from the heavy glass pitcher, filling the mug to a foamy top.

"Thanks." Lane sipped the brew under the foam.

The jukebox flipped a new 45" onto its internal record player, and the mellow opening of "American Pie" by Don McLean flowed under the sound of the diners talking.

Jenny looked over the table, full of mirth. "Okay, you got to hear this. It's jazz! James was telling me about what his little sister did to him."

"Jenny, come on now." James looked down at the wet drink ring on the paper placemat from his mug.

"Oh, it's funny. One day, James crashed really hard, and his little sister went to work on his face," Jenny said.

"It's more like I crawled through my bedroom window and passed out," James said, feeling bashful.

"What did she do?" Lane looked sideways at James.

Kyle exhaled and finished his beer in a gulp.

"She used their mom's lipstick and rouge and made him up like a glam rocker." Jenny blurted.

"Oh, no." Lane tried to picture it. *James is way too masculine for that.*

"Yeah." James blushed. "The worst part is that I woke up and sat down at the kitchen table with my dad, looking like Ziggy Stardust."

Jenny put her hand to her mouth as she giggled.

Kyle chuckled. "I bet your old man dug that."

"No." James recalled, "He went off and said, 'What kind of sissy thing have you done, boy?'"

"That's messed up," Lane said.

"He was truly pissed off." James sipped his beer. "He was going to hit me with his belt. Theresa stopped him, telling him it was a joke."

"You must've been a sight." Jenny sipped through her straw and spat out soda in a fit.

Kyle chuckled, vibing with her goofiness.

"You have no idea," James said with a forced laugh.

Lane snickered, his lip twitching. His awkward expression caused James to laugh for real. Jenny giggled, while Kyle shook his head and smiled. The waitress startled them, setting down a piping-hot pepperoni pizza on a small metal stand. Seeing the table in order, she dropped the check.

"Thanks, I got it." James picked the handwritten bill up, digging a ten-dollar bill out of his jeans.

Kyle's eyes wandered from James to Lane as he was mulling something over in his head, and he said, "Your old man seems like a mean one."

"He sure is," James said, sitting back.

Lane looked at Kyle, trying to figure him out.

"What I'm saying is he should've toughened you up." Kyle judged the two of them.

James hardened his look. "He sure has."

"Good." Kyle nodded.

Lane gave Kyle a questionable look, and he got a subtle shrug in reply.

"Do you want to split?" Kyle turned to Jenny.

"Yeah." Jenny leaned in and kissed Kyle lightly on the lips, then asked, "Lane, have you talked to Tammy?"

"I ran into her earlier." Lane held back. "She was running errands, I think."

"Tammy is always on the run." Jenny shook her hair out. "Did she mention anything about my parents?"

"It's cool. She's covering for you," Lane said in a lower voice.

"Thank god. I don't know what I'd do without her," Jenny said, relieved.

Kyle stood up and put out his hand for his girl. "Come on, babe."

"Bye, boys." Jenny rose all perky and excited.

"See you, Jenny," James said, with his mouth almost shut.

"See y'all later." Lane knew what was coming next.

Kyle leaned in and sharply said, "Take your time getting home."

"Will do." Lane watched the doting couple walk out the door. *Should've toughened you up?*

"Dig in, man." James pulled a piece of the pizza off the rack, blowing on it before biting into the end.

"Right on." Lane grabbed himself a slice. *What did Kyle mean?*

"It's hot." James pulled back and chewed slowly.

The jukebox switched to "Knocking on Heaven's Door" by Bob Dylan. Over the song, Lane heard Kyle's Challenger start up and rumble out of the lot outside. As the engine noise faded, he let go of his nagging thoughts.

James looked up from biting the pizza and stretching the cheese. "So, is this our first date, Lane?"

"What?" Lane realized they were both on the same side of the booth. "Oh, it looks like it."

"Cool," James said, chewing up the last of the piece, savoring the tangy taste.

"I'm not moving." Lane dared. "I'm comfortable right here."

"Fine by me." James refilled both of their mugs. "Drink up."

Lane took a sip. "So, what else did Jenny have to say?"

"You know, this and that." James swallowed a pepperoni. "And maybe they're running out on their own soon."

"Really?" Lane shook his head in disbelief. "There's a lot Kyle ain't telling me."

James's eyes widened as he gulped some draft to wash down the almost burning second piece he bit into. "That ain't the half of it."

Lane stopped mid-bite, tasting the salty, torn pepperoni. "What else?"

"Jenny thinks Kyle knocked her up." James snickered.

"No way. He told me he had barely gotten to third base at the drive-in." Lane took a drink of beer. "No wonder Kyle seems stressed."

"How long have they been going out?" James chewed another mouthful.

"Not long... Just a couple of months." Lane picked off a pepperoni and put it in his mouth.

"See, it happens." James kneed Lane under the table.

"Not to me!" Lane smiled.

"Good to know." James took a sudden, sincere turn. "Man, I really am grateful for you letting me stay."

"Me too. I mean, no problem." Lane felt lost in James's blue eyes again. The feeling was like a kind of hypnosis.

James knew the power of his attraction, but he could not fight feeling the same way for Lane. "How do we get to this airport?"

Lane smiled. "Look out there," he said, pointing out the window across the pines. "That road goes straight there, up to this fence, where we can park and watch planes take off and land."

"Seems simple enough." James followed the road in his imagination.

"Straight shot." Lane invited temptation. "It's supposed to be really cool at night."

"I bet it is." James let himself succumb.

Under the table, their legs pressed against each other, and their hearts raced.

SEVENTEEN

THE BSA LIGHTNING MOTORCYCLE pulled up to the ten-foot-high, chain-link fence behind Hobby Airport. Lane backed off the bike, stretching his legs out as he walked up to the fence's edge. He heard the gravel crunch, and he felt James's presence next to him.

In the distance, lights of the air traffic control tower slowly spun, somehow in sync with the other white and blue lights that spanned the runways. Through the fence, a passenger plane rolled along one runway, practically alone, with a few other planes docked at faraway terminals. The plane turned onto a second runway strip facing the fence, where Lane and James watched in silence as it slowed calmly with little lights blinking along its steel frame and wings.

A loud hum wound up into a roar as its engines powered up to full. The plane sped up faster and faster as it came straight at them. Before it reached the end of the runway, the plane took flight, lifting into the air close enough to touch.

Lane admired the majesty of the plane as it passed overhead, brownish gold with a fat red stripe and a bit of orange from its bottom to its tail.

James looked up in delight. "Oh my god, that was amazing! I've never seen one take off before!"

"It's beautiful, man!" Lane watched the twinkling craft soar higher into the night sky, like a spaceship to the stars.

The moon was waxing full, lit eerily dark and silver. Lane looked at the tight structure of James's face and felt compelled to move closer. James's blue eyes appeared darker next to the sparkling airfield.

"It definitely is." James looked back at Lane, and his smile faded into something else.

Lane's heart beat faster as boundaries broke, and he kissed James on the lips. Under the roar of the departing plane, James kissed him back in force. They roughly bumped the motorcycle as their inhibitions fell. Hands explored as they groped and kissed, tongues deep. They pulled apart, panting, the heat and taste of each other lingering.

Lane felt scared but excited. "Wow."

James looked around at the glimmer of the airport lights, then refocused. "Let's go home, Lane."

"Home." Lane nodded and followed James to mount the bike. *There's no turning back now.*

The ride was a blur, a dream that he wished would never end.

In the early 1970s, teenage runaways were common. It was a time when it was not difficult to hitchhike across the country with only a dream and a few dollars. Runaways were apt to join communes (the last vestiges of free love) or attempt to carve out a new life on the streets. Most runaways eventually wandered back home, but some truly disappeared without a trace.

Law enforcement was lax in following up on missing person cases, offering little legal recourse, and sometimes showing prejudice and indifference. In the Heights, the police told grieving family and friends that kids run away all the time, and there was nothing they could do about it.

Tattered missing posters, nailed to telephone poles, would be all that remained of some of those supposed runaways until the summer of 1973.

PART 2

2020 Lamar Drive

EIGHTEEN

SOMETIME AFTER MIDNIGHT, THE dark red Plymouth GTX rested in front of the ordinary house. Music came from within, muted by the walls.

No one was inside the living room, where the music was louder. Iron Butterfly's "In-A-Gadda-Da-Vida" rocked out, straining the speakers of a transistor radio. The room had a disheveled feel, with empty beer cans and cigarette ashes on the coffee table. In a wooden holder in the smoky room, strawberry incense burned toward the end of its stick.

A commotion, a frenzy of noise, came from another part of the house. A muffled scream rang out under the music. A rhythmic thumping fought for dominance with the beat as metal rattled against wood.

In the backroom, the suntanned teenage hitcher gasped as he was thrust against the plywood board, arms apart, each wrist hand-cuffed to a rope that went through holes in the wood. The assault stopped, and he prayed it was over. Opening his eyes, he saw the nude backside of the man who had picked him up hitchhiking as he walked out of the room. The scruffy guy he sort of remembered from the couch was shirtless in the corner, staring at him. The music made it all feel surreal.

The hitcher's vision went black, and he struggled as it returned in a gray haze. Glancing down, he saw blood flowing down from between his bare legs. On the floor were a tool chest, glass rods, and an 18-inch double-sided dildo. He tried to speak, but no words would come.

The man with the fire in his eyes returned. The cuffs rattled on the wood as the man gripped the teen's throat. The hitcher's body arched and turned as the pressure tightened. He fought the restraints, but there was no escape. Under the bass guitar, there was the sound of choking. The grip intensified, and something snapped. The noises stopped, leaving only the trippy music.

Through an archway, a dim light shone on a hallway passage. A rustling sound echoed out. Bare feet strained for traction on the wooden floor, while bare arms and hands pulled a dead weight wrapped in plastic. The covered body slid slowly from one side to the other. The chorus of the song played on as a second pair of bare feet rushed past the barren hallway.

Inside the cage, Tony stirred as the door opened, bringing rock music into the garage. His head was pounding. A grunt issued forth, and shadowy shapes dragged a body wrapped in plastic onto the cement floor. Hands on the bars, Tony stifled a scream, recognizing the half-covered face of the teenage hitcher. He cowered, realizing he might be the next victim.

Feet pounded the wooden floors of the house on Lamar Drive, followed by the sounds of putting things away. The music clicked off, and a heavy door slammed, leaving a restless silence in its wake as the incense burned out.

PART 3

SWIMSUIT BOYS

DREAM II

THE DUNES STOOD SENTINEL to the crashing surf with the sun deep in the blue sky, giving off a phosphorescent orange glow. Its light seemed farther away, more akin to the light of a full moon.

The sand was hot on Lane's bare feet while he roamed the barren beach in his swimsuit. The sandy wind thrashed his skin as he scaled the nearest dune, his feet sliding down with each sinking step. Lane struggled his way to the top in time to see James appear out of the dense air, similarly swimsuit-clad. As they closed the gap, the sand shifted underfoot.

The wind paused in anticipation, and the dune became firm. Under the darkening sky, strange, colorful blue and turquoise lights lit up the surrounding air like fireflies. Skin glistened with sweat as James's blue eyes stared evenly into Lane's browns.

A faraway bell tolled, and the fight began. Lane did his best to ward off James's strength. Flesh slid on flesh as they wrestled in a sweaty mass, each trying to take control. Their slippery skin made wrestling holds difficult to maintain. Lane almost slid free, but James had him. Fear of the unknown passed through him. There was no escape, but a gentle calm before the rough storm brought a realization to Lane. He did not want to escape.

The thought rang clear. "This is something more—this is the chaos promised."

The sky swirled into a mass of shooting stars. In a rush, Lane and James pulled off their swimsuits and collided. The feeling was so intense that it seemed to last forever, yet it was over far too quickly to satisfy the newfound urge. James backed away and lay on his side, reveling in the eyes of Lane, who stretched out the opposite way on the now softening dune. Blowing sands returned, blurring the vision. Lane positioned an arm to hold up his head, while James reached down, letting his fingers graze the edge of his sex. Stillness under assault preserved the perfectly shared moment.

The winds increased, blowing more sand across their naked flesh. Lane felt he could not move, which he found strangely comforting when he saw James immobile and calm. The sky darkened with a sandstorm, and the dunes rose in height. Their bodies transformed into less defined, statuesque clay replicas.

Something disturbed Lane under sleep paralysis. The sound of the sloshing shovel dug into the dream as the sea breeze slowly eroded the boys' clay bodies, marring their images. Sensation faded, features disappeared, and the digging continued. A relentless wind wore away the clay into dust, leaving behind mound-like shapes that used to be the lost boys.

NINETEEN

LANE AWOKE COVERED IN sweat and turned over to see James sleeping in the same pose as in the dream. The image disturbed yet stirred him. The familiar hiss of the needle stuck on the dead wax of a record (sounding like sand in the wind) distracted him. Slipping out of bed naked, he reached down to the floor for his pants, then thought twice about it. The sound crackled as he stepped over to the record player nude. The needle spun on an album, Townes Van Zandt's *High, Low and in Between*, and he moved it to the first song, "Two Hands", turning the volume lower.

Lane looked back at an equally naked James and whispered, "Am I still dreaming?"

Rolling onto his back, James opened his eyes and grinned, but his lips turned down at the sight of the door. "Is it locked?"

"Of course it is," Lane said, excited at being naked with the window half-open.

"Then get over here." James nodded, enjoying the attention.

Lane slid into bed and felt the warm touch of James's skin next to his own. Pulling his eyes away from James's blues, he let his gaze linger over his masculine form. Unlike the dream, their bodies remained solid—firm flesh, not shifting sand. He touched James's chest, making sure.

"That's better." James kissed him.

"What's your last name?" Lane felt spit on his lips.

James reached over and touched Lane's abdomen, lightly stroking muscles with the tips of his fingers. "Daly." He traced the letters D, A, L, and Y. "That's what I'm stuck with."

"James Daly, I like it," Lane said, lost in the blue eyes again.

"Well?" James tilted his face with a hint of mischief. "Are you going to tell me what yours is?"

"Oh, it's Bowden." Lane blushed for no reason.

"Alright, Lane Bowden, what's for breakfast?" James asked.

"Anything you want, man," Lane said.

James curled his lip. "Anything?"

"Come on." Lane began to move away.

James stopped him. "Whoa, hang on a moment."

Lane liked the firm touch that held him back. "What's doing?"

James leaned over and kissed Lane. "This is."

Lane breathed heavily and boldly kissed back, forcing himself to pull away. "Let's eat before you get me in trouble."

"You mean both of us," James said, a little self-conscious of the window.

"You want some boxers?" Lane opened a dresser drawer, causing the record to skip and continue on a different lyric.

"Since when do you have boxers? I didn't know you owned a pair of underwear," James said.

Lane turned and tossed a pair of white boxers onto the bed. "I'm just full of surprises."

"That you are... That you are." James pulled Lane close, his boxers only halfway up.

"I've got to see if Kyle has left." Lane felt his blood rushing south.

James breathed heavily into Lane's ear and whispered, "Outside of this room, we're pals, nothing more."

"Yeah, I guess so." Lane felt a pang of loss at the reality of the situation.

James watched Lane slide his boxers up, puzzling over something in his head. "It's the only way. We're not like those guys."

"What are we like?" Lane wondered aloud.

"We're different." James struggled to get his pair of boxers on.

"You're still queer to me," Lane said.

"Speak for yourself." James tapped Lane on the chest. "See if the coast is clear."

"Whatever." Lane crossed the room, unlocked the door, and said, "You liked it."

James moved in with a smile, putting a hand on the door. "Nobody has done that to me before."

"Really?" Lane stuttered.

"And I liked it a lot," James whispered.

"I hadn't done it either," Lane said, unsure of how to act. "It was the coolest."

"It was." James exuded sex.

Lane opened the door and peeked out into the darkened room. Straightening up, he walked toward the kitchen, turning to see James leaning against the frame watching him.

"Quit dallying around and get over here." Lane motioned.

"Funny, man." James lowered his arm and walked over.

Lane felt an ache in his chest—a feeling he had never felt before. He let James pass him into the tiled kitchen and whispered in his ear, "I knew you liked it."

"You have no idea," James whispered back.

The moment was electric and taboo outside of the bedroom.

Lane broke away and opened the refrigerator, amazed at all the extra food inside—more of everything, including beer. "Wow! How did this get in here?"

"What?" James looked inside, and a small light shone on his surprised face. "Damn, look at all the food. We don't need groceries for a month."

"There's a note." Lane picked up a folded piece of paper under a package of meat and read it.

Hey, guys, I know Kyle has been behind on rent lately, so we went and filled the fridge with groceries. It's the least we can do.
—Jenny

James palmed the note away. "So you think they're going to split soon?"

Lane took the note back and reread it to himself. Looking from the torn piece of paper to James's face, he crumpled it. "Screw it. Let's eat."

"Right on!" James dug into the refrigerator.

After two clicks, flames burst out of the stove burner. Bacon sizzled, eggs scrambled, and bread plated as they made breakfast together in no time. Lane watched James eat and wondered about the strange domestic simplicity of the scene.

"It's good," James said in between bites.

Lane asked, "What were you going to do if your old man kicked you out and we never met?"

James choked on a bit of bacon. "I would've run away."

"Just like that?" Lane marveled.

"I've had a bag packed for months." James swallowed. "I knew it was coming one day."

"I wish I could leave." Lane looked closely at his plate. "My mom's sick with cancer, and I have to see it through."

"Is she up at Heights Hospital?" James asked.

"The one and only," Lane curled his lip at the thought of it. "I hate that place."

"Yeah, hospitals give me the creeps." James got up from the table and shuffled across the tiled floor to get some clean glasses from a rack on the drainboard.

The sound of running water reminded Lane of the dream. "It gives me the creeps, too."

James filled the glasses from the faucet tap and asked, "You don't have any coffee?"

"Nah. It looks like everything except coffee," Lane said.

"I'll have to get us some; nothing like a cup in the morning." James looked disappointed.

"Sure, I guess." Lane caught the change and added, "Usually, I just smoke a joint."

"Aw, man, you got one?" James perked up.

Lane wiped his last corner of bread across the plate, shoved it in his mouth, and mumbled, "Sure do."

James wolfed down the remnants of his breakfast in two bites and followed Lane into the other room.

Kyle's space was dark, with the overhead light doing little to illuminate the gloom. Lane squatted down and reached under the twin bed, pulling out a metal drive-in food tray filled with loose weed and a lone pack of Zig Zags.

In front of the small, lifeless Zenith television, James watched Lane break a bud up on the tabletop. "Is this your weed?"

Lane scooted back a little in his folding chair, looked up from sorting stems, and grinned. "We share this."

"Cool." James spotted a stray blue pill on the floor. He picked it up and asked, "Do you share this, too?"

"What?" Lane snatched the pill. "Oh, I found some of these in his stash."

"You were snooping around his stuff?" James asked.

"No." Lane saw James's doubting look and confessed. "Well, yeah... Kyle has been acting strange, so I went and snooped. I don't think he's working at Trident anymore."

"So he's dealing." James shook his head. "Why the hell did he need some pills from me, then?"

"He's trying to hide it, but I've seen him and Don passing things to each other," Lane said.

"No wonder Don is always avoiding me. I thought it was his chick." James scratched his balls through his boxers and sat down. "Well, it's probably a little bit of both."

Lane dropped the pill, and it clanged on the tray. He pinched some weed into a loose sheet of paper, licked the sticky side along the edge, and twisted it into a joint. "Man, it smells like a locker room in here."

James stood and crossed the room, pulling back a homemade curtain to open a window. "Gotta let some air in."

Lane shoved the tray back under the bed and opened another window, creating a breezeway. He breathed in and said, "Much better."

The wind blew the curtain sheets back, causing light patterns to play across the cluttered room. Outside, a midnight black '67 Chevy Impala idled in the lot. The sound of its big block V8 engine drifted up to them on the breeze.

"This is cooler than being at home," James said. He glanced out the window and saw the outline of a scruffy teenager behind the wheel but couldn't make out his face as the car moved on. "Hey, do you see—"

"Let's smoke in the kitchen." Lane lit the joint, took a hit, and then passed it.

"Okay." James exhaled a cloud of smoke, forgetting about the car, and his eyes seemed far away for a moment. "I'll wash the dishes."

Lane looked him over with wonder. "You're just full of surprises."

"I am." James grabbed Lane's arm. "And you're going to help."

Lane took a toke. "How about we just rinse them off and take a shower?" he asked, breathing out smoke.

"Now that sounds mighty fine," James said.

"Yeah, it does." Lane let James guide him to the sink.

The lingering aroma of bacon made the kitchen smell nice. The faucet took a moment to heat up but quickly became hot enough to sterilize the dishes. James moved in closer and motioned for Lane to put the joint to his lips as water cascaded off a plate. Lane watched James take a drag of smoke from his hand, feeling the sensation of the heat from the water and of their close bodies. Lane took a quick hit and offered it back to James, who shook his head. He ground the joint out and turned the faucet off to drip. They stared at each other wordlessly in bare skin and boxers.

Thoughts of fear and desire raced through Lane's mind. He ignored one, followed the other, and grabbed James's hand, leading him to the bathroom and locking the door.

Rays of sunlight warmed through the small, barren window, but the tile was cool on their bare feet. James reached back, not breaking eye contact, and pulled the shower curtain open. Hooks scraped and chimed as they moved along a metal rod. Lane turned the shower on. Testing the water, he felt it warm up fast. Boxer shorts hit the tile as Lane and James stepped into the torrent under the showerhead. The curtain closed, and steam and water enveloped them.

Lane tried to turn, but James stopped him with an eager, almost desperate look. "No, you stay right there."

"Okay." Lane faced the white and green tile, feeling his nervous heartbeat. Water splashed over him, and he remembered the dunes. *I don't know if this is a dream or not.*

James lifted a bar of Ivory soap from its ceramic holder and lathered himself up. "It's your turn." James pressed forward.

"Goddamn, James." Lane panted. Lost in sensation, his palm clenched the tile, fingers squeaking as moisture trails dripped down. *I never imagined it to be like this. So right.*

Downstairs, Billy got out of the midnight black '67 Impala and walked around to the front of the Ben Hur Apartments. The summer breeze rippled the water in the pool as he passed it. Billy wore his leather jacket in the Texas heat because it made him feel invincible, even with the bruises and wound in his side. He had found the place by asking around; now he needed to know which apartment. Closer, he went behind the cement and iron stairs to the mailboxes. Some had labels, and some did not. His breath caught in his throat until he saw #19 with Bowden / Steiber stenciled on the paper insert. Relief washed over Billy as he ran his fingers through his sandy blond hair.

Now he could tell *them* where Lane Bowden lived, and maybe that would be enough.

TWENTY

SURROUNDED BY PINES AND live oaks, the Oak Forest Pool felt like it was in the middle of the woods. It was an illusion of sorts with houses close by through the trees. Lane was behind James, holding tight on the seat of the BSA Lightning as it rumbled up into the oil-stained parking lot. Clad in plain white T-shirts and blue swimming trunks found in the bottom of James's Navy duffel, they looked like brothers.

Life is so much easier getting around on a cool ride. Lane dismounted in the warm sunlight.

"Look at all this." James positioned his bike in the lot, kicking down the stand.

"Whoa, this is wild." Lane checked out the action.

Some crazy guy car-surfed past them in the lot, and James nudged Lane to watch the cream-colored '73 Oldsmobile Delta 88 as it turned around for another go. They both busted up at the sight of a red-haired, freckled, teenage boy hanging on top of the hood while his maniacal, dark-haired friend, with a boxer's nose, tried to turn the steering wheel fast enough to throw him off. The

Edgar Winter Group's "Frankenstein" boomed out of the radio as the car passed.

"This is one happening spot." James smiled.

"It sure is." Lane watched the car turn.

The freckled boy stood up on the hood, trying to get his balance as the car took off. He surfed to the end of the lot and dove to the side as his friend ground the gear into reverse. Lane and James's mirth faded under the blazing sun.

"Damn, I left the towels on the back of the bike." James nudged Lane and then walked away from the ruckus.

Catching sight of the dark red '68 GTX hardtop sitting idle on the far end of the lot, Lane took little notice of his departure. In a trance, he watched a brown-haired teenage boy leave his friends and walk toward the waiting GTX. There was something up with that car, the way it just kept appearing everywhere. It was...ominous. Lane felt shivers and then instantly shook them off, thinking he was being stupid.

Still, the teenager's look drew him in, and his eyes roved up from the brown cowboy boots, along the dark blue corduroy pants, to rest on the khaki shirt. He nodded at the irony of the red, white, and blue peace symbol with "USA" inside the design. The pants hung low from the tied shirt, and Lane noticed a pair of Catalina swim trunks with vertical red, turquoise, gold, and dark blue stripes showing. He fixated on the colorful free spirit, who seemed drawn to the darkness lurking inside the car. He wanted to warn the boy, but he backed up in slight horror and hit something solid and metal.

The door of a dirty white '65 Ford Econoline Van rushed open, and Lane found himself face-to-face with a man with wild eyes.

Lane gasped as he felt the world change around them, becoming slightly darker.

"Sorry, I didn't mean to startle you," the man said and smiled in a disarming way.

"No, I just backed into your van, man," Lane said.

Subtle and deliberate, the man moved closer. "Do you want to hear a joke?"

Lane wanted to look away, but something was mesmerizing about the man's eyes. The sound of the hollers and splashes from the pool dimmed in his ears, and he said, "Sure."

"A man sunbathes in the nude and ends up burning his johnson. So his doctor tells him to ease the pain by dipping it in milk," the man said, inching even closer.

Lane wanted to move away, but he felt stuck inside the shadow of the van.

"Later on, his blonde girlfriend finds him with his pecker in a cup of cold milk and remarks, 'I always wondered how you guys reloaded those things.'" The man, now in the doorframe, chuckled, his eyes on Lane.

Lane weakly grinned, backed up a step, and lied, "That's pretty funny."

The man reached out slowly and, through his charming smile, asked, "Do you want to go party?"

Lane shook his head, confused. "No. I..."

"Hey, space ranger." James broke the tension.

Lane breathed out. "What?"

The smile never left the man's face as he receded into the shadows of the van's interior.

"Let's swim." James pulled Lane away.

"Oh yeah," Lane said, snapping out of his murky thoughts.

"Later," James said to the man in the van.

Bare teeth showed through the forced smile as the man shut the door, and the sounds of the pool returned.

"Who the hell was that?" James asked.

"I don't know. I saw the red GTX, then he started talking to me, and I spaced out," Lane said.

"You got to watch yourself." James shook his head, holding the towels. "Where's the car?"

"It's over there." Lane pointed, noticing the dirty white van ease out of the parking lot.

James assessed the dark red muscle car, seeing a couple of teens smoking a joint in front of it. "I can't even see who's inside."

"It still freaks me out." Lane got a chill and looked away.

"Don't worry, I got your back," James said.

"Or vice versa." Lane flinched from an expected punch that did not come.

James nodded. *"Or vice versa."*

Tires peeled out, and the music from the car speakers returned with the surfers. Lane followed James to the pool. Looking back, he saw the footloose boy in the cowboy boots crawling into the backseat of the GTX.

James nudged his arm as they walked. "We'll build up your tolerance yet, young man."

"Hey, I can hang." Lane kept up with the pace.

"We'll see," James smugly said.

An iron gate wailed as James pushed it open, and he walked in with Lane. A cacophony of noise hit them full force, leaving the parking lot music behind them barely audible.

Teenagers and kids with little parental supervision were splashing and yelling—some even screaming in the churning water. In different ways, the youth dove from two boards with more eagerness than grace. The line for the diving boards was fairly long, yet steadily moved. Minor chaos erupted at the sides, with some pulling themselves out to jump in the pool again.

Lane and James kept their distance, moving past the splash zone. On the other side, they found a sea of flesh on display, with older teens tanning on long sun chairs in double rows near the fenced-in perimeter of the concrete pool.

Don sat watch on the pool's lone lifeguard stand, wearing his official red shorts. Red striated patterns marked his light-skinned legs—the telltale signs of jellyfish stings. Sunbathing near the lifeguard stand, Melissa, Troy, and Angie were animatedly talking about something—some private joke.

Lane felt self-conscious with James at his side, like their secret was obvious. He shrugged it off to the effect of the pot they smoked earlier.

Ignoring the trio, James nodded toward the stand. "Might as well talk to Don first."

"Right on." Lane said, swallowing his words with cottonmouth.

"I hate it when Troy and Angie are here," James said.

"Why so?" Lane asked.

"They seem like they're always talking trash." James stepped over the corner of a towel.

"We're probably the ones they think are so funny," Lane replied, copying James's sidestep.

"Maybe." James eyed the group.

"I'm just saying." Lane leaned in.

"Or maybe you're still paranoid." James touched Lane's biceps.

Lane flinched. "Quit fooling around."

"There's no fun in that." James caught Lane with his eyes.

"Whatever." Lane averted his gaze.

A chubby, seven-year-old girl cannonballed into the pool, splashing their feet.

"Bombs away!" James yelled.

Lane backed up and bumped a reclining chair with his leg, startling a long-haired, bikini-clad girl.

"Hey, watch it, man," the girl said, adjusting her layout.

"Sorry," Lane apologized, and out of the corner of his eye, he saw James laughing.

"You're a riot." James smirked.

Lane shrugged it off and followed. They approached Melissa, who was sporting her tight green bikini, from the beach. She stopped mid-conversation and stared, diverting both the raven-haired beauty, Angie's, and the golden boy, Troy's, attention.

Don noticed the difference. His whistle dropped from his lips, and he yelled, "Hey, Ollie, watch the stand!"

"I got it, Don," a tanned, lanky teenager yelled back and ambled over from talking to some girls to take over lifeguard duties.

"Cool, I won't be long." Don descended the ladder, flinching with each step from his leg wounds. "What's doing, James?"

"Not much. We just came to catch some water and rays," James said.

Don looked at them both curiously. "Hey, Lane."

"Hey, Donnie, how's the leg?" Lane asked.

Don glanced at his marked skin. "It still hurts a little."

"I know how to make it feel better." James hooked his thumbs into his swim trunks and pulled them down a little, exposing the edge of his pubic hair.

Don's eyes widened. "Hey, you stay away from me."

James let the shorts snap back, fighting a grin.

"It's not funny, man." Don glanced around.

Lane was amused until he saw Troy, Angie, and Melissa staring at them and changed his tone. "Don, there's something I've got to ask you."

"What's that?" Don pushed James, who was creeping close. "You stay back."

"Alright already." James backed off and looked curiously at Lane.

"Kyle isn't working at Trident anymore, is he?" Lane laid it out there.

Don avoided his eyes and nervously dragged his toe across the concrete. "I don't want to talk about this here."

"Aw man, I knew it!" James pulled Don's arm toward the iron fence, and Lane followed.

Melissa sat upright on the pool chair, but Angie stopped her from getting up, while Troy just stared harder.

Don smiled at Melissa. Hanging onto his fake grin, he asked, "What are you doing, man?"

"So, it's true." Lane nodded.

"What are you talking about?" Don asked, trying not to look back, knowing that there were eyes on them.

"You're both dealing." James poked Don with his finger. "And that's why you cut me out of the picture."

"It ain't like that," Don said.

"Sure it is." James pointed at the surfer and the girls. "Hell, I thought it was them."

"You're cool, man." Don said in a low voice through clenched teeth, "It's just money."

"Damn, that's messed up." Lane felt disgust at being right.

"Don't spread it around," Don begged.

"No worries. It is what it is, pal." James lifted his right foot off of the concrete, relieving the little indentations in his skin from the cement.

"You could've told us," Lane said, his voice low and hurt. "We're not narcs."

"You don't get it. Those people are hardcore," Don said seriously, although he was still grinning. "It's some kind of crime syndicate."

"Right." James shook his head in disdain. "You're telling me those freaky hippies and that weird old man are hardcore criminals."

"Not so loud," Don warned. "People disappear."

Lane remembered the missing poster on the telephone pole and inwardly shuddered.

"Whatever." James let go of Don's arm.

Melissa motioned, and Don waved her off, mouthing, "Just a minute."

"Syndicate?" Lane whispered to James, who shrugged.

"Look, promise me you won't talk about it to the girls," Don said, his eyes wide and pleading.

James shook his head. "I ain't making any promises."

"It's cool. Y'all can do whatever you want." Lane thought peace was better than conflict and started to walk away.

"Fine, but you better talk to Kyle yourself," Don said behind him.

Lane stopped and turned back. "Later, I'll do that later." He wasn't sure he would, not with how Kyle had been acting lately, and with his situation with Jenny.

"I should piss on your leg for the hell of it." James snapped the waistband of his shorts onto his skin.

"No, man. Be cool." Don inched away.

"So, is Tony involved?" Lane pivoted.

"I haven't seen that cat since the beach." Don eyed them warily.

"I thought he hooked you up." James stepped on Don's bare foot.

"He did, but now we're in. You know how strange..." Don allowed his words to fade.

Lane finished for him. "Yeah, Tony always vanishes for days to pop back up later, out of nowhere."

James moved his foot, and he and Don shared an awkward moment.

Remembering Tony getting in the dark red '68 GTX on the streets yesterday, Lane's mind flashed to the teenager in cowboy boots leaning in the window of the same car right outside the pool, in the parking lot, not long ago.

"I've got to get back to work." Don seemed anxious.

"Anyways." James stared hard. "I just wanted to clear things up since I'm staying at Lane and Kyle's now."

"You are? Oh shit... Okay, that makes sense." Don hid a smile, seeing his friends in a different way for the first time.

Lane shifted a little at this, but James didn't seem to notice. He was about to ask what, exactly, made sense when Ollie yelled from the lifeguard stand, "Hey, Don, hurry up!"

"Coming!" Don yelled back. He looked from Lane to James, then said, "Let's hang out on Thursday. I got the day off, and I'll make it up to y'all."

"Alright, see you, Don." James shook his head, smiled at the girls, and winked at Troy, who looked away.

"See you around, and watch out for the jellyfish," Lane joked.

Don winced as he walked off.

"Hey, Melissa, pleasure seeing you, babe." James waved, and she sort of waved back, looking decidedly unimpressed.

Lane nudged him, and they both caught Angie's stare and Troy's glare. The strange looks of curiosity and repulsion caused them to snicker. Fortunately, the sound of Don's metallic footsteps climbing the ladder drowned them out.

Lane flashed the peace sign. Before he realized what was happening, James tackled him, taking them both into the pool with an epic splash. The water was refreshing and heavenly against the Texas summer's sauna-like air. Oblivious to the others, they splashed, swam, and wrestled, churning the chlorinated water into thousands of tiny bubbles.

Some time later, the warm wind dried them off as the BSA Lightning motorcycle glided down a pine tree-lined road. Hanging on to James as they rode the motorcycle under the moving trees, Lane felt the swirling possibilities of what was to come.

Twenty-One

The man inside the dirty white '65 Ford Econoline van pulled off the side of the road a few blocks from the swimming pool. On the curb, the sounds of kids yelling and splashing came through the cracked driver's side window.

"He was so close, almost in my grasp." The man gripped the wheel and closed his eyes, remembering seeing Lane on the swing with the old man across from the Henley house and how he was instantly captivated.

He relived the way Lane tried to see him inside the GTX and the fear on his face. It was fate that he saw him at High Island, in the dunes. The image of him lying on the other's lap by the bonfire of the teenagers was sublime. "If it weren't for James, I would've taken him."

The flashes of hell came, and he pounded the steering wheel in the twisted agony of hate and despair. He knew that only violence could free him of its torment. In memory, he felt the rough wood of the torture board, heard the smack of flesh, and enjoyed the cutting, the shooting, the blood, the biting of genitals, and especially the strangulations as he watched his victim's eyes turn cloudy. It was ecstasy through pain. The urge burned within him. It was never enough; he needed more, more, more.

"I should have them both." He spoke softly to himself to calm the demon inside. "The boys will bring them to me, and this feeling will pass. I have to keep control. That is the key." His breathing slowed as he stared at his fiery eyes in the rearview mirror. "The other ones will have to tide me over until it is time."

The van juddered as the clutch was depressed and the gear shifted, then it cruised off to prowl the neighborhood. The man became calm and smiled, thinking about the simpler times when he gave out free candy.

Twenty-Two

Old Man Wallace's front porch was always one of the best reprieves from the heat of a summer day. Lane glanced at James, who was sitting on top of the returned Coleman ice chest. The recent memory of wrestling in the pool—surrounded by tiny air bubbles—overlapped in his mind with the image of his freshly opened beer can and the suds pouring out of the top. Thinking fast, he sucked the excess off the Lone Star, and the metallic taste of aluminum on his gums curled his lips back.

Wallace shuffled past them to take a seat in his well-worn swing chair next to Lane. "What did you say your name was again?"

James took a gulp of foamy beer and coughed before answering. "James, James Daly, sir."

"Daly, you say." Wallace scratched his chin and shifted his loose, short-sleeved shirt to the side so it breathed better. "Your father works down at Arco, doesn't he?"

"Yeah, he's worked there for as long as I can remember." James toyed with the bottom of his T-shirt, wet from the blue swim trunks.

"I worked all along the ship channel after the war," Wallace said, sipping his beer. "Hell, I even worked at Arco, except it was Sinclair Oil back then."

Lane was amazed at how Wallace seemed to know something about everyone who lived in the Heights.

Motioning to Lane, Wallace's eyes remained on James. "How did you end up with this one?"

"Hey now, he's not that bad." Lane sipped his beer, minding the foam that bubbled up.

"My old man kicked me out, and I needed a place to stay." James leaned over and dug into the freshly stocked ice chest for another round of beers.

"It sounds about right. Richard Daly was one mean, hot-headed S.O.B." Wallace took a cold one from James's out-stretched hand. "No offense, son."

"None taken. You should see my backside on a bad day." James sat back on the chest.

"Nah, keep your pants on," Lane said, staring too long.

Wallace glanced from Lane to James in realization. "So, how's Kyle with all this?"

"He's okay, I guess." Lane shifted his weight on the slow-moving swing.

"I see." Wallace mulled over his foamy Lone Star, slowing the swing to a halt.

"I'm crashing in Lane's room for now, staying out of the way," James admitted sheepishly.

"Kyle has to have his space." Lane tried to seal the breach.

Wallace chuckled, surprised he hadn't noticed before. "Listen up, boys. I'm going to tell you a story about a couple of sailors I knew once. It might be helpful...if you get my drift."

James scooted the chest closer and nodded. "I can dig it."

"Did it happen on the boat?" Lane leaned in, feeling his heart-beat and the warmth of James's arm next to his. "What was it? The USS something?"

"The USS Indiana... I'll never forget her—a BB 58 Dakota-class battleship with lots of heavy artillery. Those sailors, Ensign Sands and Calhoun, were inseparable, always poking fun. Off the coast of Okinawa in '45, we were trying to keep it clean enough to land troops from our carriers, but it was chaos. Kamikaze pilots were ramming boats in suicide dives, and my job was to blow them out of the sky from a turret at the bow. The guns were Mark 6s, 45 caliber beasts. I can still see it." Wallace's eyes misted over, lost in time.

Heat shimmered off the lawn, basking the trio in humid waves.

Lane took in the eager expression on James's face and asked, "Well, what happened, Wallace?"

"Yeah, go on." James pushed.

Sweat beaded on Wallace's forehead, and he blinked. "I could see the sailors unawares when the attack began. Sands fired up a storm at a Zero as it whooshed past, spraying the deck with bullets. In an instant, Calhoun was down. The kamikaze careened toward us. Sands let out a howl and pulled the trigger, spraying bullets all over the plane. Enemy fire cut him down, and he fell next to Calhoun. I finished off the bastard kamikaze, and he flew over in a fireball, barely missing the boat. Before it crashed into the sea, I went down to check on my mates. Blood was all over the deck."

Lane glanced at James, who bit his lip in the pause.

Wallace continued, "Calhoun held on, breathing heavily while tightly holding glassy-eyed Sand's hand. He reached into his uniform and passed me a photograph. The corpsmen were too late. Those sailors were already dead, and I watched them pull apart their bloody hands."

"Oh man, that's intense." James looked uncomfortable.

"Why did Calhoun give you the picture?" Lane asked.

"Later, I dug the photograph out of my pocket. Blood smeared the edges. It was from a photo booth. Sands and Calhoun seemed too close for sailors on shore leave, if you get my drift," Wallace said.

James looked at Lane like he was going to say something, but he bit his tongue.

Lane took a drink for courage, "Why are you telling us this story?"

Wallace sipped his beer, collating his words. "The world looks down on human nature. That's why," he said, settling back in the swing, feeling he had made his point.

James reached under his seat to get another round of beers and passed them off. "They were good sailors, weren't they?"

"Some of the best I've ever known," Wallace said.

"Then that's all that matters," James said.

"What a sad story," Lane lamented, his eyes darting to James.

"Most are." Wallace sipped his beer as he watched Mrs. Henley doing yard work on the lot diagonally across the street. "And you two best be careful of those people."

"How does that relate?" James shrugged.

Lane kicked James's shin, and the swing buckled.

"Ow!" James grabbed his leg.

Wallace breathed out as he mulled over his answer.

"You wanted to tell me something about Wayne Henley." Lane thought of the dark red GTX again as he asked, "What is it?"

"Stay away from him," Wallace warned.

"Hey, that's Don's new connection," James blurted out without thinking.

"I may be an old man, but I still have my eyes and my wits about me. I can see a lot from this porch." Wallace sighed and sipped his beer as he eyed Mrs. Henley digging in her flower bed.

"Like criminal stuff?" James wondered aloud.

"Sometimes. More often than not, it's just plain eerie stuff." Wallace let his words about the view from the porch sink in.

"I keep running into this red GTX roaming around the Heights." Lane strangely found no solace in speaking of the nagging darkness. "It creeps me out."

"That GTX belongs to David Brooks, Henley's pal. Sometimes Dean Corll is with them. That man gets under my skin. He has no business hanging out with a bunch of teenagers," Wallace said.

"The Candy Man comes over here?" James asked, amazed at the weirdness.

"Not as much as before, but I see him from time to time." Wallace solemnly swallowed a sip of warmish beer.

"So the Candy Man stuff is really true?" Lane asked, glancing at James and Wallace to see if they were ribbing him.

Old Man Wallace seemed to grow even more morose as he shifted in the swing. "The Corll Candy Company was located across the street from Helms Elementary School. He used to give the kids free candy. The shop closed after his mom moved away, but he's still hanging out with the kids; only they're a bit older than the ones before."

"I told you about that guy, the one my grandmother warned me about," James said, shaking his head.

"So, what's so strange about him partying with teenagers?" Lane felt perplexed, not liking some of his thoughts.

"Open your damn eyes," Wallace snapped as he pointed across the street. "I've seen some of those runaways over there before they disappeared."

"Maybe he just hooks them up," James said to Lane's chagrin.

"Or maybe he gets them messed up in something more sordid," Lane offered.

"Like some kind of crime syndicate." James's eyes widened.

"Whatever it is, when he's around, you can feel the vibe from here," Wallace said.

"I felt that vibe when I saw this strange man in a white van at the pool today," Lane said, feeling a haziness at the memory. His heart was beating a little faster as some of the dots began to connect. The GTX. The van. The Candy Man. The missing boys...

James glanced sideways at Lane and moved closer from his seat on the ice chest.

"The police don't care about the Waldrop brothers, Billy Baulch, Mark Scott, David Hilligiest, and Malley Winkle. They're all gone." Wallace stared at the Henley house. "The red GTX was over there earlier."

Breathing in, Lane felt his face go pale and James mouthed the word "syndicate".

Wallace continued, "I saw some teenage boy in cowboy boots step out, and Wayne made sure he got back in the car real quick. I swear they took that—"

The phone rang, breaking the tension.

"Dammit, who the hell could be calling me now?" Wallace shuffled into the house.

"Wallace's stories are weirding me out," James whispered.

Lane leaned in, whispering back, "The GTX was at the pool, and I saw the kid with the cowboy boots leaning in its window. The same car picked up Tony yesterday, and it's the same one that followed me afterwards."

"You're just tripping, man." James fidgeted with his shorts. "How come you didn't mention any of this to me?"

"I don't know. It's kind of creepy, I guess." Lane swallowed, feeling a chill under the heat. "The kids just ran away, didn't they?"

James ignored the question and asked, "Was it a dark red GTX, like the one at the beach when you were getting sick?"

"I think it's the same one." Lane felt a shock at the revelation.

James looked Lane in the eyes. "Yeah, I pulled you away, and there was somebody digging in the dunes."

"Digging, I remember the sound of a shovel." Lane felt the fear grow within him.

Wallace stepped out onto the porch with the green rotary telephone cord stretched to its limit. "It's Doctor Benway. I told him you were here."

Lane took the phone, dreading what was to come. Putting his ear to the receiver, he said, "Yes, it is." A pause. "Oh, no. Um, I will." In shock, he forgot all about the digging at the beach.

"What is it, Lane?" James sensed the change.

"It's my mom," Lane said in a daze.

"Oh, no…" James trailed off, not knowing how to finish.

"I'll drive y'all up there." Wallace pulled out his truck keys to the beat-up '55 Chevy 3100 truck from his pants pocket.

"What about my bike?" James asked.

"We'll come back for it." Lane walked with a blank face toward the truck.

TWENTY-THREE

UNSURE OF HOW TO proceed inside Heights Hospital's dank corridors, Lane looked back and saw Wallace standing sentinel with James at his side; both seemed to drift farther away down a telescoping hallway. *None of this seems real.*

With some effort, Lane pushed open the doors to the intensive care unit, and he found each area cordoned off with dividers and draped in long plastic from ceiling to floor. He was alone in the middle of the ward, surrounded by boxy electronics. The sounds of machines monitoring life signs and artificial breathing induced by respirators filled the air. A chill ran up his spine from the sights of the incapacitated patients and the icy blast of the turned-down air conditioning.

"Visiting hours are almost over." Nurse Sherry's voice seemed cold and far away "Ms. Bowden is in the third bed from the end, on the right."

Lane nodded and walked with trepidation across the shiny linoleum, each step feeling unsteady and somehow directionless. A raspy moan chilled him as he passed hidden beds, trying not to look ahead toward its source. At the end of the row, he had no choice, and the sight of his mother broke his heart.

The youthful beauty he had recently seen on his last visit had faded under a terrible strain. Parted lips in rictus, she lay motionless on the bed.

For a moment, Lane thought she might be dead, and his body trembled as something snapped inside him. "No, no, no. You can't do this."

She lay in repose as he searched for a sign of movement—a sign of life. He felt for a pulse, and her skin felt cold. The machines droned on.

Finally, he felt a faint pulse, saw the slightest rise of her chest as she stirred.

"Who's there?" She struggled to open her tightly shut eyes.

"Thank god." Lane exhaled a shaky breath. "It's me, Mom."

"Oh, Lane, I'm so glad you're here," his mom said, stirring under the sheet.

Lane felt a sense of vertigo as the room seemed to spin, and the beeping and breathing intensified.

His mom's eyes widened, and she grasped his hand as tightly as she could. "Can you take me home? I don't want to be here anymore."

Lane squeezed back, conscious of not being too rough with how delicate she had become. "Mom, you're in ICU," Lane said, and the spin slowed.

"Why? Why me?" She asked, groaning in obvious pain.

"I don't know." Lane tried to keep it together.

"I'm scared, and I'm sorry." She began to cry, and the tears flowed down her lined face. "I'm so sorry."

"You don't have anything to be sorry for." Lane looked away, but it was too late. Hot tears fell, making him feel helpless, like a little boy.

"I spoke with Dr. Benway." She sat up as best she could. "The blood tests are back. They can do the operation, and I might be okay."

The words filled the air like knives.

"I think it's worth a shot." Lane fought his mixed feelings.

"I don't like the idea of anybody cutting into my brain while I'm awake." She looked past Lane toward something beyond the walls.

Lane's eyes widened in sync with his jaw as he imagined gruesome images, adding to his shock at the state of his mom.

"I signed a release," she said softly.

Lane felt unease crawl over his skin. "When is the surgery?"

"Tomorrow morning at nine a.m. sharp," she said with a sigh of finality.

Nurse Sherry, tightly clad in her hard-starched, white uniform, appeared with a hypodermic syringe. Lane looked away as the nurse injected it into an intravenous tube and noticed the oxygen mask on the side of the bed. He opened his mouth and shut it, realizing that the drugs were allowing that brief moment with his mom.

Nurse Sherry turned on a flat heel and left without a word.

"Lane, I want you to promise me you'll take care of yourself," his mother said.

"Don't talk like that." Lane felt the anger at his helplessness rise.

She rubbed the side of her freckled face and muttered, "I'm so tired—tired of all of this."

"Me too." The entire world felt uneven in his mind.

"Hey, sport." A tall, dark-haired, olive-skinned man commanded their attention. "Hey, babe."

Lane turned to see his father, the man who had beaten him mercilessly until he abandoned them, standing at the foot of the bed. He looked out the window at the majestic oak, bracing for the confrontation.

"John, you came to see me." She brightened at the sight of her not-quite ex-husband.

"Sure thing. You called, I came," John said.

Lane's face turned red, and his lips tightened to a whitish line. "I got to run."

"Wait, Lane. Don't go. It's your father," she said with a little edge in her voice.

"Listen to your mother, boy." John smirked.

"He ain't my father, not anymore." Lane backed away. "Don't believe a thing that man says. Not one thing. Don't you dare."

John bowed up, ready to fight. "Get over here. Can't you see what you're doing to her?" He stalked closer. "It's what you've always done." Even closer, he gritted his teeth. "We should've put you in that boy's home when we had the chance."

"I'm out of here." Lane bolted, avoiding his father's long-reaching hand.

The sound of his mother's voice haunted him as he left. "Lane, please stay."

The machines beeped, inhaled, and exhaled. The doors pushed apart, and Lane jogged into James, who was still at Wallace's side. "Let's get out of here. My old man crashed the scene, and he's about as cool as yours."

"Is your mom okay?" James felt his feet itching to move.

"No, but we got to split." Lane expected the doors to swing open at any moment.

Knowing the Bowden family routine quite well, Wallace nodded. "I'll tell you what, I think I'll stick around."

"Thanks for the beer and the ride," Lane said, moving off.

"Anytime." Wallace leaned back against the sterile wall. "Take care, boys."

"Are we walking?" James kept Lane's pace.

"It ain't far." Lane grabbed James's arm and pulled him along the hospital hallway, almost tripping them both.

"Slow down, cowboy," James said.

"Not until we're out of here," Lane said, looking back over his shoulder. He didn't want to fight his father today; he'd been hit enough in the past. It was best just to get the hell out of there.

"Okay." James allowed himself to be led.

They stopped at an outdated set of elevators. The metal dials above each closed shaft showed both of the cars in the lobby.

Impatience surged through Lane's veins, and he motioned to the door for a quick escape. "Let's take the stairs."

"Whatever you say, man," James said with a manic look.

They said nothing as they descended the stairwell—footfall after footfall—until a squeaky door opened onto the oppressive summer heat.

The memory of someone calling his name in the stairwell made Lane start to bolt, but James held him back. "It's cool, Lane. We're outside."

"Right on, James." Lane looked up and saw the ominous hospital building blocking the sun. "I just needed out of there."

James followed his gaze. "Take your time... And let's not freak out."

Avoiding James's eyes out of fear of crying, Lane asked, "You want to get a drink or something?"

James sensed the moment and did not want to push it. "Sure, we can hit up the Bohemian on the way back."

"Cool, I've been pretty tightly wound lately." Lane sniffled.

James pulled Lane away from the morbid site. "Don't worry, I'm here for you."

"I'm glad you're here because this sucks," Lane said.

"Hell, this whole damn place sucks." James nudged Lane with an elbow.

The walk improved the mood, and Lane relaxed, telling himself not to worry. *There's nothing I can do till morning, anyway.*

James was naturally chipper and asked, "If you could go anywhere away from here, where would you go?"

"I don't know, California, maybe." Lane mulled it over.

"Not bad." James's eyes twinkled. "We need a plan, though."

"Where would you go then?" Lane asked.

"Mexico—down south." James let his thoughts fly. "Money stretches a lot further, and life is simple for a gringo down there."

"You're so full of it, James." Lane looked at him twice to see how serious he really was and said, "We're not going on the road like some characters in a book, man."

"Don't you get it... We could be anybody we wanted. We could be free," James said, his voice longing and dreamy.

"Maybe we could." Lane felt the pull to run away despite the ridiculousness of it all. "But Mexico is out of the question."

"Aw, why not?" James ribbed.

"We're Americans." Lane tapped his chest. "We don't belong there, that's why."

"If you say so." James pivoted. "I *am* down for California."

"One day real soon, I'll be down for California too," Lane said wistfully.

"Great, it's a plan!" James walked with a little kick in his step.

He really is serious. Hell, it's the right thing to do. "I really mean it, James. I'll ride with you to the end," Lane said, feeling his heart rush.

James's face lit up. "Awesome."

TWENTY-FOUR

TELEVISION RECEPTION CAME IN and out in waves, with static winning over. The teenage boy kicked the wooden coffee table with his boot and fanned himself with his unbuttoned khaki shirt. He was bored. *What the hell am I doing out here in Pasadena?*

Patting his dark blue corduroy pants, he was glad that his swimsuit underneath was dry. The ice swirled in the empty glass in his hand as he rose off the ratty couch. The room spun and righted itself, and he figured it was from the weed he smoked before going to the swimming pool.

Voices came from one of the bedrooms as he walked into the kitchen to make himself a fresh drink. He poured some whiskey in the glass and was startled by a whimper from a side door. Sipping the liquor, he investigated. Metal rattled from the other side. Turning the knob, he opened the door into pitch black, straining to see as his hand roved the wall for a light switch. Metal rattled, and a wheezy whine came from the darkness, causing him to back away.

Breathing out, he rationalized, *It's probably just a dog.*

Something crashed in another room, drawing his attention. The hallway seemed long in the half-light as the teenage boy crept to where the muffled voices were louder. He put his ear to the door, trying to make out what they were saying.

The words came into focus from a deeper voice and the guy whose car he had gotten into.

"Why did you bring him here so early?"

"So we could party."

"This is my house and my rules."

"All of this could end just like that."

A scuffle sounded from the other side of the door, and the argument dropped an octave to hushed tones.

"This scene is lame," the teenage boy muttered.

Curious, he walked down to a door at the end that was ajar. Through the crack, he saw plastic laid out on the floor. The teenager pushed the door, and it creaked open wider, giving him a view of the torture board. Ropes, handcuffs, and sex implements lay beside a tool chest and a three-pound metal can of Crisco grease.

"No fucking way," he said, not noticing the voices had stopped.

The glass slipped out of his hand as Wayne pushed him into the wall. "You weren't supposed to see that."

"What is all of this?" The teenage boy looked toward the doorway and saw David, the long-haired, bespectacled teen, blocking the way out.

"It's just the thing he does," Wayne said, inching closer with his arms out.

"I ain't doing this." The teen reached into his corduroy pants and switched open a blade. "Let me go."

"Whoa, it's not like that." Wayne reached and missed a swipe.

"I'll cut you. I swear to God. I will." In desperation, the teenage boy swiped the blade back and forth, then opened his mouth in terror.

Dean Corll, the man with the fiery eyes, stormed into the room, brandishing a .22 caliber gun. He pulled the trigger three times, striking the boy in the chest, head, and, as he turned, the back. Blood trickled out of the small holes as the teenager slid down the wall, the knife falling from his limp hand.

"What the hell, Dean?" Wayne looked perplexed. "He wasn't going anywhere."

"I don't have time for this." Dean glared, rage animating his fists. "Next time, you better listen to me. Now sort out this mess."

Before his teenage accomplices could reply, the phone rang and he stormed out of the room.

Wayne and David shared a look, understanding their fate if they didn't follow through on his orders. David moved the hair out of his eyes and grabbed a leg, sliding the boy onto the plastic. The teenager's head twisted to the side as his body spasmed. Wayne folded the plastic over, patting the boy's body as his last breath left.

In the kitchen, Dean's demeanor changed as he listened to the voice on the other end of the line. "You did good." A pause. "There is one last thing, though."

TWENTY-FIVE

THE BOHEMIAN ALWAYS LOOKS dirtier in the daytime. The dingy building came into view through a mirage of heat, and Lane could not believe they had traversed so much turf so fast. The sight comforted him, like it was a worn-down home away from home, even more so with James at his side.

"Look at this freaking dive." James shook his head.

"You got the first round?" Lane asked.

"No worries. The beers are on me." James traded Lane a five-dollar bill. "As long as you get the table."

"Deal," Lane said, trading some coins and crumpling the bill in his palm. It amazed him how much James calmed him.

Once indoors, it took a minute for their eyes to adjust to the smoky gloom. The Bohemian was fairly empty, except for some roughneck types sitting at the bar, downing whiskey.

Lane wondered if anybody seeing them together would guess their secret but shrugged it off as a useless worry.

The country twang of Elvis Presley's "Fool" played out of the jukebox. On the other side of it in a darkened corner, Billy hung up the payphone and watched them for a second before going outside.

James cut out to a pool table. "I'm going to rack 'em up."

"Alright, I break then." Lane turned and nodded to Ralph behind the bar, not surprised at seeing the biker owner, no matter the time of day.

Ralph ran a hand through his long white and gray beard. "What will it be, son?"

"Give me a couple of Lone Stars," Lane said.

Eyeing James as he reached inside the cooler, Ralph pulled out two beers and popped off their caps with a couple of flicks of his wrist.

Lane laid down a five. "Keep them coming for a bit."

"There'll be cold ones waiting when you're ready." Ralph tucked the bill into the cash drawer and wiped his hands on his coveralls.

"Thanks, Ralph." Lane walked across the shabby space and felt déjà vu while he watched James hang over the table, set up the rack, and then look up with his piercing blue eyes.

"All set." James shoved off from the table and grabbed a beer. "Thanks."

Lane set down his cold, sweaty bottle, chalked up a cue, and aimed to break. Feeling James's eyes still on him, he asked, "What?"

"Nothing." He waited for a second, then when Lane kept staring, he continued, "Well, are you okay, man?"

Lane nodded back, sliding the pool cue between his fingers. "Yeah, I'm cool."

"Good," James said.

The pool balls cracked a moment later and Lane smiled at sinking a couple of solids and a stripe. "James, do you think we're like those sailors, the ones Wallace was talking about?"

James scratched his side through his tight, white T-shirt and moved closer. He whispered, "Yeah, I reckon we're like them—different but lucky." He glanced at the oilfield cowboys. "Lucky not to get beaten down."

Lane missed a bank shot. The number six ball bounced recklessly, changing the layout of the table. Roles reversed. Lane watched James take advantage of a straight-on shot at the eleven in the side. "Have you ever been in a fight about it?"

"Once." James stood taller, flexing his muscles but not aware of it. "Once was enough."

"What happened?" Lane leaned in.

"I crashed at this guy's house one night." James chewed on his lip. "We were really drunk, and I did something stupid."

The door opened, and light flashed across the bar. They both looked over and saw a rough, sandy-blond street kid wander inside, eyeballing the place.

"I'll tell you later," James whispered.

Lane kind of recognized the kid. "Is that Billy?"

"Yep, he's more trouble than Tony." James tapped the bottom of his cue on the floor.

"Damn, I thought so. Do you want to split?" Lane felt edgy.

"Nah, it will be cool." James smiled as Billy approached. "What's doing, Billy?"

Lane switched the cue from one hand to the other, hoping James would take the next shot so he could shoot.

Billy brushed his bangs away from his eyes. "Well, you know how it is. You got another beer?"

"I guess." James motioned to Lane and mouthed, "Just one."

Lane dug into his pocket. "I'll get us another round."

"Have you seen Tony?" Billy asked, watching Lane step away.

Lane heard him and thought of hiding in the oleanders watching the GTX stalk Tony, but he didn't want to creep himself out again and continued on to the bar.

James studied the layout of the the cluster of balls on the table's green felt, searching for his next move. "Not since Sunday."

"Man, that cat owes me some grass," Billy said without conviction, figuring Tony was in the cage now.

James hit a combo, knocking the twelve into the ten. "I ain't seen him since."

"Figures." Billy took the cold beer offered to him.

Lane stepped back with the beers, wondering when Billy showered last. "So, where have you been hanging?"

Billy strangely eyed the door before he answered in a low voice. "Closer to town. Some crazy shit went down, and I had to change scenes."

James missed a long shot and took his beer from Lane. "Who are you hiding from now?"

"What? No one... What've you heard?" Billy's eyes flashed fear.

Walking along the table, Lane leaned down to sink a solid ball. "Nothing, he's just playing with you."

"Oh." Billy chugged his beer in one continuous gulp. "That's cool. I... I um... I wanted to ask you something."

"What's that?" James tapped his stick on Lane's, then motioned with his head for him to shoot.

"I can get some good shit if you're looking to score." Billy offered, hopeful.

"Nah, man." James twirled the cue. "We're good."

"Are you sure?" Billy looked to the door again.

"Yeah, I'm sure." James locked eyes with Billy.

"Well, I'll be around." Billy seemed jumpy as he walked off.

"Later, man." Lane felt out of place around Billy and was relieved to see him go. The nagging thought of Tony getting into the dark red GTX crossed his mind.

James sipped his beer, eyes returning to Lane as the blackened door closed. "See, that wasn't so bad."

"What scene is he talking about?" Lane asked.

"Satan's Alley." James sneered.

Lane missed his shot, almost tearing the fabric.

Holding back the snickers, James said, "That's what they call it, Satan's Alley. It's where all the dopers hang."

"Screw that, I never want to see any place called that," Lane said.

"I hear it's dangerous with rough types hanging around at all hours." James leaned over the table, ready for his shot.

"The Heights are a dump, but they're not that bad." Lane felt watched. "Why the hell would he change scenes?"

"You got me. No telling what Billy is into." James smoothly sank the eight ball into the corner pocket.

The jukebox changed over to "Satin Sheets" by Jeanne Pruett, creating a honky-tonk vibe in the Bohemian.

"Do you think I should've told him about Tony getting in that car?" Lane asked.

"Nah. Sometimes it's good to stay out of trouble's way," James said.

"If you say so," Lane mumbled, remembering Tony's face as he got into that GTX and imagining it on a missing poster. *He's just a junkie. I'm being stupid.* Popping some quarters into the slot on the pool table, he swigged his beer and focused once more on James. "I'm going to beat you this time."

"Maybe...if I let you." James joked.

"Right on." Lane sorted the balls inside the triangle rack. "What happened in that fight you were going to tell me about?"

"Oh, that." James tittered. "Like I said, I did something stupid."

"Hold on, James." Lane stood closer so no one could over-hear their conversation. "What did you do?"

"I was really drunk and got too close to the guy." James smiled in a strange, off-putting way. "I'll be damned. He swung at me and gave me a black eye."

"Worse than the one you got now?" Lane asked.

"Oh, yeah." James touched his eye. "This ain't nothing com-pared to that."

"No way." Lane felt his lip twitch. "Did he tell anybody?"

James shook his head. "I guess he didn't want anyone to think he was queer. After that, he never talked to me again. His name was Sam. We were best friends growing up, and I threw it all away in one night."

"I've thought about stuff, but I'm usually too scared to act on it—scared that something like that would happen," Lane admitted.

"Like I said, I was stupid, and it cost me. I swore I'd never try that again." James took a gulp of his beer.

"You said you'd fooled around with somebody, though." Lane tilted his head.

"Not like I have with you." James's blue eyes widened. "I feel like we're more than just fooling around."

"Oh yeah?" Lane leaned on his cue, feeling it too. He was curious, jealous, and excited all at once. "What did you do then?"

"You know stuff—stuff you usually do alone." James motioned up and down on the cue with his hand, stoking the spark between them.

"How did you know?" The idea of a hidden world fascinated Lane.

"Weeks after the fight, I found a guy who was cool with it as long as I could figure out the signs. I had to be tough and could never talk about it until I met you," James said.

"What signs?" Lane asked.

"One sign was the way you were staring me down when we first met. I noticed that and knew." James moved closer, cue in hand.

"Damn, was I that obvious?" Lane asked.

"Only to me." James switched hands. "I was checking you out, too."

"Good thing it worked out, huh?" Lane moved close enough to knock cue sticks.

"Damn straight." James clinked bottles with Lane.

Twenty-Six

THE BLACK-PAINTED BATHROOM of the Bohemian Pool Hall was grungy. The cement floor had puddles by the open urinals, and only one of the two sinks on the cracked counter worked. Billy turned on the faucet and moved a wet, shaky hand through his sandy blond hair. His skin was pale and sweaty. He had waited too long between fixes.

"One last thing," he said to the mirror, repeating what he heard on the phone. *Somehow I have to figure out how to get them to go to Graham Park.*

He twisted off the tap and slinked into a stall, shutting and locking the small bolt on its door. He sat on the toilet and stared at the dirty and colorful graffiti, waiting as someone came in, peed, and left. Untying his boot, he pulled out his kit. The process calmed him almost as much as the heroin to come.

I'm not free yet, but I have this, he thought as he plunged the needle into his arm. The rush was instantaneous, and he felt the horrors of the torture board and cage fade into unimportance.

"One last thing," he said aloud and laughed at the insanity of it all.

Twenty-Seven

THE BLACK-PAINTED DOOR OF the Bohemian Pool Hall slammed shut behind Lane and James on its steel hinges. In the fallen night, the outside parking lot was half full of cars.

"We should have ridden my bike," James lamented.

"It's cool. We don't have that far to go," Lane said.

"I guess." James looked down the road. "Which way is the fastest?"

"This way." Lane led. "We'll get your bike on the way."

As they passed the oleander bushes, a shadowed muscle car's engine started up.

Lane glanced at James. Crazy thoughts about possible futures collided with each other inside his head. *Is he the one?*

"What?" James caught the stare.

Lane ignored the rumbling engine and asked, "Are you serious about running away?"

"Yeah, like a heart attack." James's expression sobered. "I've been for a long time."

"I wish we could go now." Lane felt a pang of guilt for being so honest.

"Me too." James shuffled closer on the walk and they grazed hands and smiled at each other.

Unseen in the distance, the shadowed car followed them with its lights off.

Feeling content with James as they walked in silence, Lane led him onto 27th Street. James's face lit up at the sight of his BSA Lightning in Wallace's ramshackle front yard. "I love this bike, man."

"It is aces." Lane admired the sleek motorcycle as they approached.

"I guess we'll walk it away from his house since it's late." James kicked up the stand and rolled the bike toward the street.

The tires made a gravelly sound crossing the drive. Lane swore it sounded louder than it should. He looked around the darkened neighborhood. The Henley house taunted him with its bland windows and bent blinds.

"Are you okay?" James asked.

"That house freaks me out. It always seems like someone's watching." Lane felt a chill.

"Who cares if they are?" James guided them and his bike away.

"I'm just saying. That's all." Lane forced himself not to look back. "After all that stuff Wallace told us, it feels strange."

"I know what you mean." James got on the bike and kick-started it. "Get on."

Unaware, Lane straddled the seat behind him, and they rode on towards the Ben Hur Apartments. Hidden behind a parked car, the shadowed muscle car cruised onto the street under the canopy of long oak branches. The passenger smiled as he took in the boys' forms intertwined on the motorcycle. They were perfect.

Soon, he thought. *I'll have what I want.*

Twenty-Eight

Three Night Hawk TV dinners slid across the kitchen table, leaving tiny ice crystals to melt on their tops.

"Can we cook them all at once?" James bent up the corners of each aluminum tray for ventilation.

"I don't see why not." Lane investigated the bottom of one of his dirty feet, below his skinny legs and loose-fitting blue shorts.

"Is the temperature right?" James reached out with an icy metal tray.

Lane blocked the cold metal with his hand. "Yeah, the dial is on it. Throw them in."

James slid the trays—one after the other—into the gas oven. He shut the door, causing it to whine on stiff hinges. Heat radiated in the humid kitchen.

"Hell, the sun is down, and it still feels like this." Lane wiped sweat off his forehead.

"It is hot in here." James pulled off his shirt, leaving it lying on the back of a chair.

"And the windows are open too," Lane said as he took off his T-shirt, laying it on top of the other one. He took a moment to trace the fading mark on his stomach from the punch by Riley.

"How long are they going to take?" James twisted his body into view.

"Half an hour, or so." Lane watched him, bit his lip, and asked, "Do you want to see what's on the tube?"

"Sure." James passed close enough to brush his bare skin against Lane's.

Lane followed to the next room and plopped into a folding chair at the card table. James pulled up another chair at his side. Magnetism radiated between them. Lane reached across and pulled the TV knob, touching James's arm in passing.

The Zenith took a moment to warm up, slowly going from a gray-white screen to fade in on the scroll of *Hawaii Five-O*'s end credits.

"Damn, I like that show." James got up. "I'm going to get our beers in the kitchen."

"Okay. I'll find something to watch." Lane turned the dial, stopping on the *ABC Movie of the Week*, instantly enthralled by a blonde teenager and her diary.

James clunked a can down, beer foam sloshing out of its top. "Here you go."

"Thanks." Lane could not pull his eyes away from the screen.

"What is this?" James watched the girl on TV light a joint.

"I don't know. I guess we'll find out," Lane said.

"Aw, man, that's much better." Kyle came in the room only in a towel, fresh out of the shower.

James offered, "Hey, we popped a TV dinner in the oven for you."

"Cool." Kyle walked past, stopping to look down. "Do y'all want to burn one?"

"Damn right." James brightened.

"Uh-huh." Lane nodded, lost in the story.

Kyle tossed the towel on his bed and looked around aimlessly for a moment. Lane glanced at his body, like he always did. He elbowed James for staring, who shrugged in response. Kyle unburied another chair from a mound of dirty clothes, then retrieved some boxers and the rolling tray from under the bed.

"I knew I had one pair left." Kyle slid his found boxers over his nakedness.

The television show broke for a commercial, and the announcer stated, "*Go Ask Alice* will be back after these messages."

Lane cleared his throat and felt James tense on his side. "Kyle, I need to ask you a few things."

Looking up from de-stemming his pot, Kyle said, "Go ahead, shoot."

"Are you taking off with Jenny?" He was blunter than he'd intended.

"I'm going to check on those TV dinners." James cleared his throat and left.

Kyle sighed. "I'm thinking about it."

"Were you going to tell me?" Feeling a little upset, Lane grabbed the sides of his head.

"Of course I was, Lane. It's just difficult," Kyle said quieter.

"Shit, I lost my job," Lane said, "and you want to split?"

"James can cover my part." Kyle shoved some weed into a rolling paper.

"It ain't right, Kyle." As he watched Kyle, preoccupied with the weed, he knew his words were falling on deaf ears.

"I screwed up, man." Kyle licked the paper and twisted it. "I thought I could deal, and that hasn't worked out so well."

"Why didn't you tell me?" Lane asked.

"I don't know, Lane. You kind of weird me out sometimes." Kyle smirked.

"What does that have to do with anything?" Lane wondered if Kyle knew.

"I'm sorry this is how it's going down, but I do get you high," Kyle said.

"It ain't like that I—" A fork appeared before Lane's eyes, and he took it. "Hey, James."

"Hey." James slid the TV dinners on the table using his kitchen towel-wrapped hand.

"You still could have told me." Lane felt irritated.

Kyle burned his finger and yanked it away. "Well, now you know."

"You guys need a minute?" James seemed ready to bolt, but he handed Kyle a fork and stood his ground.

"Nah, we're good," Kyle said, ending it.

"Cool." James sat down and cautiously removed the aluminum, steam rising in his face on release. "Careful, it's hot."

"Aren't we, Lane?" Kyle dug in.

"For the most part." Letting it go, Lane peeled back the lid, seeing Salisbury steak in brown gravy, tater tots, and corn.

"Let's get high then." Kyle lit up a joint.

The threesome smoked quietly and zoned out on the flick. Lane took notice, realizing that it always seemed easier to tune out and get into a film when stoned.

On the next commercial break, James broke the silence. "Is it me?"

"Huh?" Lane asked, surprised.

"No, man." Kyle laughed, lurching back into his chair. "Actually, it's a good thing you're here."

"Really?" James took a bite. Chewing, he mumbled, "I don't want to be any trouble."

"Everything's cool." Lane hoped it was. "It still sucks, Kyle."

"I've got to get my head straight. Nothing personal." Kyle wavered and licked his dry lips. "I think I knocked up Jenny."

"You told me you haven't gotten in her panties yet." Lane rubbed his palms across his face.

"Well, damn. She let me go all the way when we first met." Kyle rubbed his chin. "After that, she just teased me."

James put his elbows on the table, almost tipping it. "When are you leaving?" The antenna swerved dangerously close, and the TV's reception turned staticky until he pushed it back in place.

"Soon." Kyle held out his hand. "I promise I'll leave you something."

"Fine." Lane reluctantly shook Kyle's hand and made peace.

Alice took her last hurrah. In silence, different thoughts spun around each of their heads as they watched the program until its bleak O.D. ending.

Kyle stepped away, lay back on his bed, and stretched out. "I'm going to crash."

"Lightweight," Lane teased as he reached for the TV knob.

"You're one to talk, little man." Kyle buried his face in a pillow.

Lane clicked through the limited channels. "The worm has turned, buddy."

"Do you even know what that means?" Kyle managed through the muffling fabric.

"Not really, man." Lane turned the dial to find a musical with sailors dancing in the streets and quickly snapped off the television, seeing the humorous gleam in James's eyes.

Under the sheet, Kyle turned his back on them.

"Nothing is on, so I guess we're going to crash too," Lane said.

"Night, Kyle." James leaned over, smacking Kyle's shoulder.

"Night, guys." Kyle closed his eyes.

Lane led the way, picking up their T-shirts before clicking off the kitchen light. They padded into the bedroom. The lock clicked, and Lane turned around to see James's handsome face in the instant before the darkness came.

James whispered, "Get over here, sailor boy."

"Aye, captain," Lane replied as they wrestled down on the bed.

PART 4

NIGHTHAWKS

Twenty-Nine

The strangers watched as the light went out in the open window of apartment #19 of the Ben Hur complex. The close figures inside had disappeared. The night was humid and sticky with a hot breeze. Water lightly lapped the sides of the swimming pool. Someone yelled down the street. The nighttime noise stopped short of the parking lot where the dark red GTX idled.

Wayne Henley, the scruffy younger driver, eyed the Challenger at the end and made a decision. "Not tonight. They're not alone."

"I want the boy I saw at the beach," Dean Corll said beside him.

"Why do you want him so bad?"

"Because it pleases me." The fire burned in the man's eyes.

"I'll get him," Wayne swore. "It won't be long now, just not tonight. It's too risky."

"And I want the boy who rides the motorcycle." The passenger whistled softly.

"I'll get him too," Wayne whispered, "for a price."

"I take care of you. I always have." Dean licked his lips. "I'm gonna have my fun."

"What about the boy from the swimming pool?" Wayne turned to face the bogeyman, fascinated by the monster.

"He can wait," Dean whispered, his words heavy with power and anger. "We'll bury him before dawn." Inside the murky interior, the man's teeth flashed like a wolf ready to strike. "Let's find someone else."

Wayne nodded in acquiescence and backed out to cruise the neighborhood, leaving Lane and James unaware that they were on the Candyman's list.

THE LAST UNIDENTIFIED VICTIM is only known as ML73-3356. The mystery of this lost teenage boy in striped swimming trunks and cowboy boots resurfaced when investigators tested his remains with new technology. He was a white male with dark brown hair, between 5'2" and 5'7", and between the ages of 15 and 20 when he died from asphyxia due to strangulation. Prison trustees under police supervision exhumed his remains from the earthen floor of the boat shed, center, back of the room, on August 9th, 1973.

No one has claimed him in all this time.

And in recent years, investigators at the Harris County Institute of Forensic Sciences have received a tip and photos of a boy named Bobby French who went missing in the timeframe of the murders. DNA testing has sorted out misidentified bodies and given names to others over time, but without a genetic sample from a relative to positively identify the remains, his fate is officially unknown.

Interred in a potter's field, John Doe 1973, aka Swimsuit Boy (ML73-3356), rests in a burial ground for criminals and unidentified persons.

Acknowledgments

It took a ton of research and a funeral to create *Summer 1973*, and I could not have done it without the people I met along the way.

I would like to thank my partner, Bo, for giving me the space to write and supporting my craft over the years. He has also championed this story in its many iterations, keeping me from taking the easy way out.

My sincere appreciation goes to David-Jack Fletcher for surprising me with a New Year's Eve email stating interest in the manuscript two years after passing on it. He has been a solid editor and has helped me shape and give balance to the material.

The seed of the story was planted when Larry Crawford gave me and a friend an after-hours showing of an exhibit of serial killer art at the Hyde Park Gallery in 1997. Elmer Wayne Henley's still-life of surreal sunflowers and his seascape with green grass growing in the dunes disturbed me as much as a victim's family member protesting by burning a painting on the street at the art opening. I had no idea I would be writing about the true crime years later.

In 2008, the case had come back in the news with new DNA evidence identifying remains and correcting prior mistakes. Crawford approached me about writing a story about the art, so I decided to learn about the murders.

There is nothing as creepy as hanging out in the Reading Room of the haunted Julia Ideson Building of the Houston Public Library. At that time, there were only two out-of-print books about the murders, both published in 1974. I found a used copy of *The Man With the Candy* by Jack Olsen, but I had to read *Mass Murder in Houston* by John K. Gurwell in the old room. Under the dim lighting, it was easy to believe ghosts walked the aisles.

Newspapers and video media were difficult to find when I started this project. I explored the library's microfiche archives of *The Houston Post* and *Chronicle*, finding stories from August 8th, 1973, when the crimes became known through the discovery of the bodies and the subsequent trials (1974–1979) of Henley and Brooks, the teenage accomplices. The 1981 mondo documentary, *The Killing of America*, had a segment about the murders, and the 2000 film *Collectors* focused on serial killer art, showing the images I saw in person at the gallery.

In researching the crimes, I had the invaluable assistance of David Babb, who worked for the Harris County Coroner and KPFT 90.1 Pacifica Radio. He helped me find all the existing true crime locations from the Heights to the boat shed and introduced me to gay activist Ray Hill. Ray had civic connections and knew a lot about the city's history even though he was in prison for jewelry theft when the story of the murders broke. I talked to him a bit about the Heights neighborhood and gay life of the time, and he even had me sit in on a live broadcast of his call-in radio program, *The Prison Show*, an outreach program for inmates and their families.

Sharron Derrick, the forensic anthropologist, could not identify one victim, ML73-3356, John Doe 1973, aka Swimsuit Boy. Through Ray Hill, I met her when I attended the boy's funeral in November 2009 at a pauper's field where they bury criminals and unidentified persons. The reconstructed photo of him at the graveside with his statistics, clothes, manner of death, and where they found him in the boat shed haunted me. I decided then and there that the story was going to be different, inspired by this lost boy.

When I was writing the first draft, I did some promotional gigs with Chris Binum, an actor who was filming *In a Madman's World*, Josh Vargas's now lost film. He played the teenage killer, Henley, and tried to get me an extra part, but I was moving to Chicago at the time. The incomplete film is notable for Marilyn Burns, star of *The Texas Chain Saw Massacre*, in her final role as Mrs. Hill, a victim's mother. So many weird connections come into play when you work on a project.

I appreciate the feedback I received from Preston Fassel when he was story editor for Cinestate, which owned *Fangoria* magazine and was producing movies and books. He encouraged me to continue to work on the manuscript by writing to me about how it was a commendable goal to take on a gay coming-of-age story set in 1973 and the importance of humanizing the victims who lost their lives. It was the best rejection I ever got from a submission.

I hope the *Summer 1973* series brings attention to the lost boys who are still missing, the ones who never ran away and ended up in a shallow grave.

About the Author

Dean Cade is a Gen X writer who survived the chaos of running wild on the streets in his formative years. Now he uses those experiences—the highs, lows, and the redemptions—to write memoir and genre fiction. A lifelong film and horror fan, he spends his free time lifting weights. Dean lives in Texas with his partner, Bo, and their Siberian Husky, Max. deancade.com.

Summer 1973 is his debut. This title is the second in the trilogy and a unique combination of true crime and horror.